Contents

CW01084937

About the author 3

Acknowledgements 4

Introduction 5

Section 1: An introduction to self-harm and young people 16

Section 2: Working with young people who self-harm 42

Section 3: Introducing suicide 56

Section 4: The epidemiology of suicide 60

Section 5: Key areas in youth suicide prevention 73

Section 6: Action learning – direct work and community responses 86

A concluding note from the author 96

Useful contacts 98

Certificate of achievement 101

DVD 102

Youth Self-harm and Suicide Awareness: A reflective practice guide for staff working with children and young people

© Jude Sellen-Cole

The author has asserted her rights in accordance with the Copyright, Designs and Patents Act (1988) to be identified as the author of this work.

Published by:
Pavilion Publishing and Media Ltd
Rayford House, School Road, Hove, BN3 5HX
Tel: 01273 434 943
Fax: 01273 227 308
Email: info@pavpub.com

Published 2015.

A catalogue record for this book is available from the British Library.

Print ISBN: 978-1-910366-37-0

EPUB ISBN: 978-1-910366-42-4

EPDF ISBN: 978-1-910366-43-1

MOBI ISBN: 978-1-910366-44-8

Pavilion is the leading publisher and provider of professional development products and services for workers in the health, social care, education and community safety sectors. We believe that everyone has the right to fulfil their potential and we strive to supply products and services that help raise standards, promote best practices and support continuing professional development.

DVD disclaimer
The Sh! film was originally produced by SHED in 2005 and commissioned by Hastings and Rother PCT. It is reproduced with permission from Hastings and Rother PCT. Jude Sellen-Cole accepts full liability for the inclusion of the video in this guide and any queries can be directed to her via Pavilion Publishing and Media Ltd.

Author: Jude Sellen-Cole, Impact Wellbeing

Editors: Catherine Ansell-Jones and Jan Alcoe, Pavilion Publishing and Media Ltd

Cover design: Phil Morash, Pavilion Publishing and Media Ltd

Page layout: Emma Dawe, Pavilion Publishing and Media Ltd

Printing: CMP Digital Print Solutions

About the author

Jude Sellen-Cole has worked in health and social care since 1982 where her roles have included practitioner, operational manager, commissioner and senior policy officer. In these roles she has primarily focused on meeting the mental health needs of children, young people and their carers. Jude has specific skills and knowledge in understanding suicide, depression, addiction, eating disorders, aggressive behaviours and self-harm. Jude is an accredited social worker and a trainee Transactional Analysis psychotherapist. She has a long-running column in *Mental Health Today* magazine.

Since 2002 Jude has worked as an independent young people's mental health advisor and trainer. She currently runs one and two-day bespoke mental health training courses for frontline staff across the UK. Jude has been involved in supporting the development of local self-harm protocols and youth suicide prevention strategies in various regions. She has extensive experience in strategic commissioning and acts as a consultant to local areas to support multi-agency child and adolescent mental health services commissioning arrangements.

This guide brings together the materials Jude has collated over the years, which she uses to support her ongoing work.

Jude is the founder of Impact Wellbeing, a social enterprise set up to tackle the impact of trauma and build resilience in children and young people. You can find out more at: www.facebook.com/impactwellbeing.

Acknowledgements

This guide would not have been possible were it not for the service users – children, young people, family members and adult survivors – I have worked with over many years, along with the feedback I have received from an amazing variety of professionals and support workers from across the country, who have given their time and energy to attend courses and group discussions which I have facilitated. Their views about what is and isn't useful in facilitating learning and self-nurturing have helped to shape the information in this guide.

Particular thanks go to Martin Gilbert and Amanda Daniels in Birmingham and all the wonderful staff I have had the privilege to work with there. And equally, thanks go to Janet Johnson from Hounslow and the numerous staff across Hounslow children's services who have attended my training days. Many of whom are an inspiration to us all due to their capacity to open their hearts and minds to examine ways to support the young people they work with.

Thanks also goes to the amazing children's residential workers who, day in, day out, care for some of the most distressed and unhappy children, with compassion, commitment and an energy that continues to astound. Thank you to the children's local authority residential staff in North East Lincolnshire and London.

Introduction

'It is not the depth of my cut that's indicative of my mental distress.'
15-year-old girl

The author has collated feedback from numerous staff seeking to support young people who self-harm (including self-injury, suicidal ideation and attempted suicide) across the UK from 1998 to the present date. Feedback shows that while it is useful for staff to attend training courses which provide facts and figures on self-harm and suicide, this approach alone does little to build professionals' confidence. Leaving a training day knowing that every 30 minutes a young person tries to take their life (Sellen, 2009), that two children in every classroom self-harm (MHF, 2006) and that ice cubes and elastic bands can be useful harm minimisation techniques, does not address the attitudes that a professional may hold about self-injury and/or suicide.

This practical self-development guide seeks to recognise the importance of acknowledging our own attitudes and encourage workers to understand how their attitudinal stance impacts their work with young people who self-harm or feel suicidal. Having the opportunity to reflect upon the impact of our attitudes is an essential part of developing a positive working relationship with a young person and it can optimise future work with them. It also serves us in our own professional development to ensure that we, too, are taking care of our emotional health and development. Equally, you will have the opportunity to consider a wide range of facts and research about self-harm and suicide.

Repeatedly staff ask for more opportunities to reflect on their practice, but in contrast, instead receive increased case management reviews, which they do not feel adequately meet their needs. Recent years have seen an increase in practice managers and advanced social work practitioners following on from the Munro recommendations (see ChildLine, 2014), yet many of these roles are filled by experienced staff who tell me they are 'learning on their feet' when it comes to advising staff and making sense of the increasing numbers of children and young people who are self-harming and expressing suicidal ideation.

Human relationships are key to the delivery of effective services, but they are often overlooked.

Crowther and Cowen (2011) identified the following qualities and skills as being fundamental:

- maintaining a child-focused approach
- achieving an effective balance of support and challenge
- being open, clear and direct
- building trust and mutual respect

- empowering and enabling service users
- demonstrating action-focused practice
- being able to interact well with children and young people
- presenting information in ways that service users can understand.

Who is the guide for?

This guide is written for those working with children and young people in an education, social care, youth justice or healthcare setting. Staff in these settings are likely to know of, or be directly offering support to, a child or young person who is distressed.

Many staff will know of children and young people who manage their distress in destructive and harmful ways. Some of these children may seem unable to regain their place in the world as individuals who experience hope and happiness, and staff may see them spiralling into despair. The impact this can have on professionals can potentially be profound.

This guide gives the reader the opportunity to explore:

- why a child or young person might self-harm
- why a child or young person continues to self-harm
- why children and young people consider suicide
- why children and young people take their life by suicide
- what to do if a child or young person takes their life by suicide

- what local communities can do to support a child or young person sooner.

It will enable staff to ask questions like:

- Should I be doing anything else?
- Am I getting it right?
- Is it true that talking about self-harm or suicide in schools encourages it?
- How do I, as a professional, take care of myself?

The guide is for multidisciplinary staff who want to explore these questions and expand their existing knowledge about the complex area of self-harm and suicide among young people.

What are the outcomes of using the guide?

The benefits of using the material in this guide have been evidenced by the repeated feedback received by the author from staff across the UK.

Outcomes include:

- increased understanding of why people self-harm
- increased understanding of their own emotional processes provoked in relationships with service users and others
- introduction of new tools to enhance communication
- provision of an evidence base to support professional development
- provision of opportunities to discuss the challenges faced in this complex and often distressing area of work

- familiarity with the NICE Guidelines (2011) *Self-harm: Longer term management* (Clinical Guideline 133) and responsibilities (in health and social care in particular) regarding the application of these guidelines
- a framework for action regarding suicide prevention and responses to youth suicide
- skills in separating out facts, aspirations and myths about self-harm and suicide
- a portfolio of reference materials and resources to build upon.

Context

'Self-harm is one of the top five causes of acute medical admission in the UK each year. In the year after attending an emergency department about one in six will self-harm again and nearly 1% will die by suicide.' (RCPsych, 2006)

In October 2014 The Royal College of Psychiatrists updated their guidance on managing self-harm in young people. The report, *Managing Self-harm in Young People* (CR192), replaced *Managing Deliberate Self-harm in Young People* (CR64), which was published in 1998. The 2014 report provides updated guidance on managing self-harm in young people up to the age of 18, in line with the children's National Service Framework (Department of Health, 2004). This includes young people who have learning disabilities.

Self-harm can be considered as a spectrum of behaviour ranging from occasional self-scratching, to taking an overdose with an intent to die, to completed suicide. In synchrony with the National Institute for Health and Care Excellence's (NICE, 2004; 2011) guidance, the 2014 Royal College of Psychiatrists' report does not cover broader aspects of self-harming behaviour such as harmful drinking, other types of risk-taking behaviour or self-injurious behaviour (a term typically used in the field of intellectual disability, referring to behaviours such as head banging or self-biting).

Rather than focusing on professional responses to clinical need, the report primarily addresses broader matters such as professional roles and links, and pathways between professionals. It also addresses service arrangements and links between services. It does not cover the management of self-harming behaviour in in-patient psychiatric settings.

The report sits among several other reports, including NICE guidance on self-harm (NICE, 2004; 2011), the national suicide prevention strategy (DH, 2012), best practice in risk management (DH, 2007), advice on discussing self-harm with young people (Cello & YoungMinds, 2012), a College report (CR 158) on helping people who self-harm (Royal College of Psychiatrists, 2010) and the implications for public health practitioners of self-harm by young people (NSPCC Inform, 2009).

It is largely recognised that children's services professionals feel uncomfortable and lack confidence in supporting children and young people who self-harm (MHF, 2006; Sellen &

Haddad, 2010). Self-harm, indeed, provokes a wide range of strong emotional responses.

A growing body of evidence suggests that alcohol and substance abuse are second only to depression and other mood disorders when it comes to risk factors for suicide (Clay, 2009). In one study, alcohol and drug abuse disorders were associated with a six-fold increase in the risk of suicide attempts (Clay, 2009).

Too frequently, we associate a correlation between self-harm and suicide, yet service users repeatedly explain self-harm is more commonly experienced as a strategy for survival. In contrast, on examining the profiles of people who have taken their life by suicide, the need to increase awareness about the correlation between alcohol and substance misuse and suicide must be a priority. Many young people self-medicate and/or self-injure to manage their mental distress. While the focus of the training is the latter, it does consider risk factors such as alcohol and substance misuse to support the sections of this guide on suicide awareness.

It is equally acknowledged that on examining the risk factors precipitating a person who takes their life by suicide, the presence of self-injury may be found; however, service users would encourage us to hold in mind that the act of self-injury is, for the most part, motivated by the desire to survive. This is a position well documented as early as 1938 by Karl Menninger: '...the impulse toward self-destructiveness is examined as a misdirection of the instinct for survival, a turning inward of the aggressive behaviour developed for self-preservation...' (1938).

The International Association for Suicide Prevention (IASP), in collaboration with the World Health Organization (WHO), is raising awareness among the scientific community and the general population that suicide is preventable. Public health awareness and education campaigns have often focused on the role of risk factors in the development of suicidal behaviour. In order to increase effectiveness in preventing suicide, IASP proposes our efforts should not only be towards reducing risk factors, but also towards strengthening protective factors, with the aim of preventing vulnerability to suicide and strengthening people's resilience.

Suicidal behaviour has become a major public health problem across the world. It is a complex phenomenon that usually occurs along a continuum, progressing from suicidal thoughts to planning, attempting suicide, and, finally, to dying by suicide.

Data from the WHO indicates that approximately one million people worldwide die by suicide each year. This corresponds to one death every 40 seconds. The number of lives lost each year through suicide exceeds the number of deaths due to homicide and war combined (WHO, 2012).

Suicide attempts and suicidal ideation are far more common; for example, the number of suicide attempts may be up to 20 times the number of deaths by suicide. It is estimated that about five per cent of people attempt suicide at least once in their life and that the lifetime prevalence of suicidal ideation in the general population is between 10–14%. Suicide is one of the leading causes of death in the world and over the last year rates have increased by 60% in some countries (WHO, 2012).

ChildLine's report, *Can I Tell You Something?* (2014), found that the number of young people calling the organisation about self-harm increased by 41% from 2013 to 2014. This was the second year running that the number of calls had increased.

Where age was known, 70% of the contacts ChildLine received about self-harm came from young people aged between 12–15 years. In addition, there was a 33% increase in young people talking about suicidal thoughts and feelings. For 16–18 year olds, suicide was the third most common reason for contacting ChildLine. While 17 year olds are the age group most commonly affected by issues relating to suicide, the biggest increase year-on-year was among 12-15-year-olds (ChildLine, 2014).

Policy context

The Department of Health's report *Preventing Suicide in England: A cross-governmental outcomes strategy to save lives* (2012) states that suicide is a major social issue. It states that suicides are not inevitable and there are many ways that services, communities and society can help prevent them.

The strategy's overall objectives are:

- a reduction in the suicide rate in the general population in England
- better support for those bereaved and affected by suicide.

The report identifies six key areas for action to support the delivery of these objectives:

1. Reduce the risk of suicide in key high-risk groups
2. Tailor approaches to improve mental health in specific groups
3. Reduce access to the means of suicide
4. Provide better information and support to those bereaved or affected by suicide
5. Support the media in delivering sensitive approaches to suicide and suicidal behaviour
6. Support research, data collection and monitoring.

High risk groups are identified as young and middle-aged men, people in the care of mental health services, people with a history of self-harm, people in contact with the criminal justice system and specific occupational groups such as doctors, nurses, veterinary workers, farmers and agricultural workers.

Preventing Suicide in England: A cross-governmental outcomes strategy to save lives (DH, 2012) makes the following recommendations.

- Those who work with men in different settings, especially primary care, need to be particularly alert to the signs of suicidal behaviour.
- Treating mental and physical health as equally important in the context of suicide prevention will have implications for the management of care for people who self-harm, and for effective 24-hour responses to mental health crises.

- Accessible, high quality mental health services are fundamental to reducing the suicide risk in people of all ages with mental health problems.
- Emergency departments and primary care have important roles in the care of people who self-harm, with a focus on good communication and follow-up.
- Continuing to improve mental health outcomes for people in contact with the criminal justice system will contribute to suicide prevention, as will the ongoing delivery of safer custody.
- Suicide risk by occupational groups may vary nationally and even locally.

It is vital that the statutory sector and local agencies adapt their suicide prevention interventions accordingly.

Working definitions

It is important to define the terminology used in this guide.

This guide uses the National Institute of Health and Care Excellence's definition of self-harm:

'The term self-harm is used in this guideline to refer to any act of self-poisoning or self-injury carried out by an individual irrespective of motivation. This commonly involves self-poisoning with medication or self-injury by cutting. There are several important exclusions that this term is not intended to cover. These include harm to the self arising from excessive consumption of alcohol or recreational drugs, or from starvation arising from anorexia nervosa, or accidental harm to oneself.' (NICE, 2011)

The guide uses the World Health Organization's definition of suicide: 'Suicide is the act of deliberately killing oneself. Risk factors for suicide include mental disorder (such as depression, personality disorder, alcohol dependence, or schizophrenia), and some physical illnesses, such as neurological disorders, cancer, and HIV infection. There are effective strategies and interventions for the prevention of suicide.' (WHO, 2012)

It is also useful to consider Menninger's definition of suicide: 'Suicide is an escape from an intolerable life situation. If the situation be an external, visible one, the suicide is brave; if the struggle be an internal, invisible one, the suicide is crazy' (Menninger, 1938).

What is reflective practice?

Before considering the practical aspects of the content of this guide, it is important to clarify the model of reflective practice that underpins it. The importance of making learning explicit from experience has been well researched and evidenced (see Honey & Mumford, 1992).

According to Honey and Mumford (2000):

'Everyone learns from experience but, rather like breathing, too often is taken for granted and carried out intuitively without even realising it. The snags with learning intuitively are that you:

- aren't clear about what you've learned
- cannot communicate your learning to other people

- *don't know what you learn and therefore cannot improve the process and become a more efficient learner from experience*
- *do not help other people to learn from their experiences.*

These are strong omissions and it is strongly suggested that intuitive learning needs be supplemented with learning that is conscious and deliberate.'

The sections in this guide adopt a learning cycle model to encourage the reader to take a model of reflective practice into their learning environment ie. work settings with children and young people.

Reflective practice encourages the practitioner, manager and commissioner to enter into open communication with service users by recognising the service user as the expert by experience, while providing the professional with an increased awareness of their own confidence and the capacity to work with a service user to make sense of the service user's experience.

What is Transactional Analysis?

The International Transactional Analysis Association describes Transactional Analysis as *'a thematic psychotherapy for personal growth and personal change'* (ITAA, 2012). The basics of Transactional Analysis (TA) structure and inform this guide. Some models from Transactional Analysis are introduced in this guide to support your working relationships with young people who self-harm and/or express suicidal ideation. The author,

who is a trainee TA psychotherapist, has continually received positive feedback from participants on how accessible and useful the TA concepts are. The concepts provide a greater understanding of the strong emotions provoked within us when trying to support a young person who self-harms, and the emotions provoked within a service user.

TA Today: A new introduction to transactional analysis (Steward & Joines, 2009) is a very useful starting point in introducing the models of TA. The basics of the following concepts are considered.

The lifescript: This explains how our present life patterns originated in childhood. TA develops explanations of how we may continue to replay childhood strategies in grown-up life, even when these produce results that are self-defeating or painful.

Ego-state model: This helps us to understand how people function and how they express their personality in terms of behaviour. An ego-state is a set of related behaviours. If a person is behaving, thinking and feeling in response to what is going on around them and using all the resources available to them as a grown-up, they are said to be in their Adult ego state.

The other two ego states are known as Parent and Child. The former resulting in behaviours induced by certain stimuli, resulting in a person copying the behaviours of their childhood carers (be these negative or positive); the latter is when a person returns to the behaviours they adopted as children. Again, usually provoked by certain stimuli, be it another's behaviour towards them or an environmental factor.

The Drama Triangle: Stephen Karpman (1968) suggested that people can provoke emotional responses in one another and that they often occupy one of three dominant positions in relation to each other. He referred to these positions as the persecutor, the rescuer and the victim – the detail of this model is unpacked in Section 1: An introduction to self-harm and young people. It is this particular model – and the subsequent model, the Winner's Triangle – that participants find most helpful in making sense of the emotions provoked in response to self-harm and youth suicide (see Section 1).

Structure of the guide

The guide comprises six sections:

- Section 1: An introduction to self-harm and young people
- Section 2: Working with young people who self-harm
- Section 3: Introducing suicide
- Section 4: The epidemiology of suicide
- Section 5: Key areas in youth suicide prevention
- Section 6: Action learning – direct work and community responses.

The information and activities in each section encourage the reader to explore, focus and develop their understanding and skills in working with young people who are experiencing emotional distress.

Section 1 introduces self-harm in young people and Section 2 expands on this learning by examining more closely working with young people who self-harm. Both sections are underpinned by a framework of reflective practice and a basic application of theories from Transactional Analysis. Irrespective of the reader's level of experience and knowledge, it is recommended that you read both sections. The rationale for this is that, despite Section 1 offering an 'introduction to self-harm', the content takes the reader through a process that encourages opportunities for increased self-awareness with regard to the subject matter and professional practice. Section 1 also introduces some of the key concepts that underpin the learning in Section 2.

Sections 3, 4, 5 and 6 are designed to increase the reader's knowledge and understanding about suicide. It is important to acknowledge the high level of stigma and the strong emotional responses that thinking and talking about suicide can evoke. It is anticipated that one of the outcomes for readers working through these sections will be to take the learning and look at developing local youth suicide prevention guidelines and support within their local areas and organisations.

The development of local conversations along with action is needed to address the sad reality that some children and young people see no other choice but to kill themselves. Children's services are keen to put in place proactive measures to reduce suicide and develop postvention strategies. This guide aims to support that process.

Sections 3, 4, 5 and 6 encourage a closer dialogue between children's services and professionals to consider what strategies they currently have in place to i) identify the distressed child, ii) respond iii) consider how accessible provisions might be for the child who feels suicidal, and iv) consider how well informed staff feel about the subject of suicide.

Other considerations

Emotional support

The information and activities in this guide focus on increasing understanding about suicide and the idea that self-harm is perceived by many service users as a means of survival. Suicide and self-harm are distressing to both professionals and service users. This can result from emotions that are evoked and/or as a result of discussions that remind participants of particularly distressing times in their own lives. It is recommended that before completing the activities within this guide and/or reading it, you ensure you take care of yourself and know who to contact if you feel vulnerable.

Safeguarding, self-harm and youth suicide

Connecting With People (2012) provides some useful information sheets that were originally written for GPs, but are very useful for anyone working with children and young people who self-harm or express suicidal ideation.

(You can access them at: http://www.connectingwithpeople.org/sites/default/files/SuicideMitigationInPrimaryCareFactsheet_0612.pdf)

During the course of using this guide, you may want to consider specific situations involving children or young people. The following paragraphs provide brief notes on dealing with some specific situations.

In addition, you may wish to take forward in your local areas recommendation 10 in *Managing Self-harm in Young People* (CR192) (RPsych, 2014), which explores joint protocols for the management of self-harm.

Self-discharge from A & E

What should be done if a child or young person who has been admitted to A & E with self-inflicted injuries or attempted suicide self-discharges?

If the medical situation is life threatening, the child's case should be discussed with the consultant paediatrician or psychiatrist and involve children's social care and the police. If the child or young person self-discharges before a mental health assessment is done, it is recommended that social care and health work in collaboration to support the child or young person in the community. Ideally, all areas should have a self-harm multi-agency protocol. This provides a framework to offer clarity to professionals, the service user and families regarding expectations of all parties, interventions and resources available, timeframes and projected measurable outcomes. (See recommendation 11 in *Managing Self-harm in Young People* (CR192) (RPsych, 2014).

Child protection and safeguarding

What should be done if a child or young person discloses abuse, or if you suspect abuse?

Abuse is a generic term that covers the ill-treatment of children and young people, whether it is physical, emotional or sexual harm, or where the standard of care provided to the child does not adequately meet their needs. If you suspect abuse, or where abuse is disclosed to you, stay calm and be sensitive, record all observations and conversations with the child, and follow the child protection and safeguarding protocols for your organisation.

Responding to a child or young person who has self-injured or who is feeling suicidal

What should be done if a child or young person shows evidence or expresses an intent to self-harm, or where they disclose suicidal ideation?

The child or young person should be spoken with immediately and it should be ascertained whether they have taken any substances or injured themselves and, if so, the appropriate care should be given. A supportive and non-judgemental attitude when talking with the child or young person is important as it can help to ascertain what may be

troubling them and what support or help they might need. It is important to explore to what extent self-harm is imminent or planned.

When can confidential information about a child or young person be shared?

Informed consent to share information should be sought if the child or young person is competent, unless the situation is urgent and there is not time to seek consent or seeking consent is likely to cause serious harm to someone or prejudice the prevention or detection of serious crime.

If consent to information sharing is refused, or can/should not be sought, information should still be shared when: there is reason to believe that not sharing information is likely to result in serious harm to the young person or someone else.

References

Cello & YoungMinds (2012) *Talking Self-harm*. London: YoungMinds and Cello. Available at: http://www.cellogroup.com/pdfs/talking_self_harm.pdf (accessed January 2015).

Clay RA (2009) *Substance abuse and suicide prevention: evidence and implications: a white paper*. SAMHSA January/February 2009 **17** (1) 8–9.

ChildLine (2014) *Can I Tell You Something?* London: ChildLine.

Connecting with People (2012) *Suicide Mitigation in Primary Care*. Available at: http://www.connectingwithpeople.org/sites/default/files/SuicideMitigationInPrimaryCareFactsheet_0612.pdf (accessed January 2015).

Crowther K & Cowen G (2011) *Effective Relationships with Vulnerable Parents to Improve Outcomes for Children and Young People: Final study report*. York: Consulting for Action for Children.

Department of Health (2004) *National Service Framework: Children, young people and maternity services*. London: DH.

Department of Health (2007) *Best Practice in Managing Risk: Principles and guidance for best practice in the assessment and management of risk to self and others in mental health services.* London: DH.

Department of Health (2012) *Preventing Suicide in England: A cross-governmental outcomes strategy to save lives.* London: DH.

Honey P & Mumford A (1992) *The Manual of Learning Styles.* Maidenhead: Peter Honey Publications.

Honey P & Mumford A (2000) *The Learning Styles Questionnaire 80-Item version.* Maidenhead: Peter Honey Publications.

International Transactional Analysis Association (2012) *About TA* [online]. Available at: http://itaaworld.org/index.php/about-ta (accessed January 2012).

Karpman S (1968) Fairy tales and script drama analysis. *Transactional Analysis Bulletin* 7 26.

Mental Health Foundation (2006) *The Truth Hurts: A national inquiry about self-harm.* London: MHF.

Menninger K (1938) *Man Against Himself.* New York: Harcourt.

National Institute of Health and Clinical Excellence (2004) *Self-harm: the short-term physical and psychological management and secondary prevention of self-harm in primary and secondary care* (CG16) [online]. Available at: http://www.nice.org.uk/guidance/cg16 (accessed March 2015).

National Institute of Health and Clinical Excellence Guidelines (2011) *Self-harm: Longer term management* (Clinical Guideline 133). London: NICE.

NSPCC Inform (2009) *Young People Who Self-harm: Implications for practitioners.* London: Reconstruct Research Service.

Royal College of Psychiatrists (1998) *Managing Deliberate Self-harm in Young People* (CR64). London: RPsych.

Royal College of Psychiatrists (2006) *Better Services for People who Self-Harm: Quality standards for healthcare professionals.* London: RPSYCH.

Royal College of Psychiatrists (2010) *Self-harm, Suicide and Risk: Helping people who self-harm.* London: RCP.

Royal College of Psychiatrists (2014) *Managing Self-harm in Young People (CR 192).* London: RPSYCH. Available at: http://www.rcpsych.ac.uk/files/pdfversion/CR192.pdf (accessed January 2015).

Sellen J (2009) *See Beyond the Label: Training pack.* London: Young Minds.

Sellen J & Haddad M (2010) *Improving the Quality of School Mental Health: A quality improvement evaluation for school nurses & teachers (QUEST): A Health Foundation funded research project to develop and evaluate mental health care within secondary schools.* London: Institute of Psychiatry at King's College London, Rethink, Sutton & Merton PCT, Charlie Waller Memorial Trust.

Steward & Joines (2009) *TA Today: A new introduction to Transactional Analysis.* Nottingham: Chapel Hill.

World Health Organization (2012) *World Suicide Prevention Day: Facts and figures* [online]. Available at: http://www.iasp.info/wspd/pdf/2012_wspd_facts_and_ figures.pdf (accessed February 2013). (See also http://www.iasp.info/wspd/powerpoint/2014/2014_wspd_powerpoint_facts_and_figures.pptx for a more recent set of facts and figures).

Further resources

Impact Wellbeing (2013) *Youth Suicide: A reality* by Jude Sellen.

Section 1

An introduction to self-harm and young people

Introduction

This section explores self-injury, its prevalence and its relationship to other self-harming behaviours. It offers an opportunity to reflect on personal attitudes and how these can invite both positive and/or negative outcomes in our working relationships.

It explores the demands and difficulties of working with vulnerable children and young people and offers strategies to promote good mental health and to manage self-injury through better support and harm minimisation. It also considers the NICE guidelines for the long-term management of self-harm (CG 133) and their implications for working practice.

How often do you have the opportunity to reflect on your own attitudes and practice? And how often can you acknowledge the enormity of the skills and knowledge you bring to work each day? The answer is usually rarely. This is despite repeated research and professionals' requests for further training, adequate supervision and reflective practice. It seems that not much has changed since the findings from the Mental Health Foundation's report *The Truth Hurts: A national inquiry about self-harm* (2006).

Developing a positive and supportive working relationship with a young person who self-harms is frequently experienced as being difficult by many professionals. This section provides opportunities to unpack personal attitudes, as well as to explore those of young people.

It can be helpful to think about how an attitude comes into being. Oppenheim (2000) argues that there are three components that construct an attitude:

- cognitive
- emotional
- action tendency.

The following text provides an opportunity to consider Oppenheim's three components by first examining perceptions and understanding of self-injurious behaviours, including:

- assumptions and interpretations about self-harm behaviours
- verbal and non-verbal expressions about self-harm behaviours – positive and negative responses

- the need to be aware of our expressions and what we may or may not project onto a young person.

Professionals working with children and young people who self-harm can make common assumptions and perceptions, which lead to interpretations of the child or young person's behaviour. Such interpretations lead to professionals expressing, either verbally or non-verbally, attitudes about the behaviours presented to them. These can be both positive and negative. It is important to understand this so that you are aware of what you may or may not be projecting onto the young person.

What is mental health?

It is important to consider our understanding of mental health as a concept. People will have a range of views and perceptions about why young people self-harm. Some may think it is due to a psychiatric disorder and others may think, or be working with staff who think, it is an attention-seeking behaviour. It is important that we look at this in more detail first before exploring other themes.

Activity: What is mental health?

In the first column of the table, write down the first few words that come into your head when you hear the term 'mental health'. Aim to put any sense of political correctness aside for now.

Then clear your mind by thinking about something different eg. chores you need to do, your plans for the weekend.

Next, in the second column, write down the first few words that come into your head when you hear the term 'physical health', again using any words you want.

Mental health	Physical health

Have a look at what you've written. Most people tend to write negative words on hearing or seeing the words 'mental health', often words associated with mental ill-health, and positive words about physical health.

'Even my teacher says that my brother's "mental" just because he's got ADHD. So if they are saying stuff like that, how are the kids in my class going to change?' Young carer, aged 14

The word 'mental' is seen and frequently used almost exclusively as a negative word. It is often used as a word of abuse in the playground, at work and even within the family to scorn or make fun of another. And yet, without mental health, we would arguably achieve and enjoy very little. As the public health mantra says, there is 'no health without mental health'.

As we are both mental and physical beings, our mental health is just as important as our physical health. In order to fully enjoy life, have a sense of self-worth and achievement in our personal, social and working worlds, we need to recognise and care for both our mental and physical health needs.

Good mental health isn't just the absence of mental health problems.

Mental health is mental well-being. It is having:

- a sense of personal well-being
- a capacity to form mutually satisfying relationships with others
- being able and prepared to adapt within a normal range of psychological and social demands appropriate to a given stage of development

Reflection

How is the word 'mental' used in the media?

What do you do when you hear the word 'mental' used in a derogative way?

Reflect on any experiences you have had of negative and positive views held by both colleagues and young people you work with.

- an ability to learn new skills appropriate to age and developmental competence.

Experiencing mental health problems is part of everyday life when we feel sad, worried, unhappy or fearful, and these feelings are sometimes very normal and healthy responses to trauma, loss and/ or abuse that we might experience.

However, for some, these feelings can become entrenched, we can become stuck and we may need the support and help of mental health professionals.

On average, one in four of us will experience a mental health problem in the course of a year. Fortunately, the majority of people who experience mental health problems can recover from them and learn to live with them, especially if they get help early on.

Unfortunately, many people experiencing a mental health problem don't receive the right kind of help and some don't receive any help at all. In fact, many people with mental health problems are shunned or discriminated by their families, friends and the professionals who are supposed to care for them.

Ensuring we embrace the positive use of the words 'mental health' can help people talk about their feelings more openly, so that when they are in need of additional support they will not be fearful of being shunned or chastised, but realise that help will be at hand and perceived as a normal part of taking care of a person's health. Mental health is no different from experiencing a physical knock/accident in which a person needs rest and support to get back on their feet.

Activity: How do you determine seriousness?

If we accept that our relationship with the young person who self-injures is the key tool in our work, it is equally key to examine the attitudes we take into any relationship with a young person who self-injures. This activity invites you to consider the factors which influence your attitudes and how, without adequate time for self-reflection, you will take these into the relationship.

Number the following items in order of seriousness, interpreting the terms for yourself.

- Chronic overworking and insomnia
- Cutting arms
- Gambling
- Bingeing and vomiting
- Smoking cigarettes
- Drinking alone

What are the factors that have influenced your decisions?

What process did you go through to arrive at your chosen order of seriousness?

What were your gut feelings and how did they impact your attitudes and decision making when making judgements about the severity of risk?

Ask one or two colleagues to give their views on the ordering. Do these change your view?

The perceived seriousness of self-harm

Many workers who do the previous activity conclude they had not thought that self-harming behaviour could include these other behaviours, but they can see how other behaviours could be interpreted as self-harm eg. sexual risk taking and the overuse of sport etc. Some workers place them in an order of severity, but most cluster them and/ or put them in a circle seeing them as possibly having similar weight.

Other points which come up include the following:

- Some raise the importance of social norms and how these influence our thinking.

- Many have not considered the internal damage to the organs that bulimia can cause.

- Many realise the extent to which their own personal experiences shape their interpretations of severity, professional and personal concern regarding another's behaviours.

- Some participants ask questions about whether tattooing and piercing are self-harming behaviours.

- Some participants ask whether self-harming behaviours become addictive behaviours.

Self-injuring can focus attention on the short-term impact due to the physical nature of the harm (eg. scars, burns,

Reflection

What might the impact be on how we perceive the young person if we interpret their behaviour as 'coping'?

cuts being visible). The worker focuses on whether they can still see cuts etc. and also experiences relief when there are no further signs; though this may lead to relief for the worker, it is not necessarily indicative of a 'relief' from the often long-term causal factors that have led to a young person self-injuring.

This guide introduces the concept of 'mood alteration', challenging the concept of self-harm as a 'coping mechanism' as limiting and disempowering in working with young people.

Coping strategy vs. mood alteration

This sub-section focuses on a narrower definition of self-harm ie. self-injury, rather than considering the wider range of self-harming behaviours that were covered previously. It will help you to examine the importance of a professional's relationship with a young person. While risk assessments and questionnaires may invite discussion about self-injurious behaviour, your relationship with a young person is the most crucial tool. However, this fact is often overlooked unless the person is a therapist.

A respondent's relationship with a young person who self-injures will be affected by their own assumptions, attitudes and judgements about self-injury. These will be conveyed in verbal exchanges and through their body language. As professionals, we hold emotions in our own internal and external landscapes. For example, young people who self-injure are communicating via their external landscapes ie. through the markings, cuts, scars and bruises on their bodies. Many websites and information leaflets on self-injury frequently refer to it as a coping method or strategy. This viewpoint can create an unhelpful dynamic between a professional and a young person and will be further examined later.

Developing a working relationship with a young person who self-harms is not about becoming a 'mini therapist', but about being a professional who is trying to make sense of why a young person may be self-injuring. For example, examining the importance of what may influence the young person and enabling them to experience a relationship where there is open and supportive communication.

By viewing self-injurious behaviour as a strategy for altering mood rather than as a coping strategy, a professional's perception of a young person will hopefully change. This, in turn, will affect the professional's relationship with the young person, which will hopefully become more positive and constructive.

In doing the next activity, you may find it difficult to move away from viewing self-harm as a coping mechanism, to

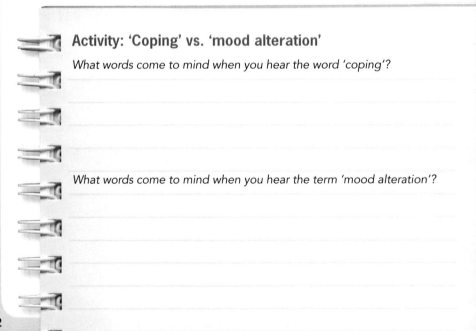

Activity: 'Coping' vs. 'mood alteration'

What words come to mind when you hear the word 'coping'?

What words come to mind when you hear the term 'mood alteration'?

one in which a young person uses self-harm to alter their mood. This may be because it is a new concept. Understanding self-harm as a way to understand mood is key as it focuses on the main tool you have when working with an individual – your relationship. The understanding you hold about the rationale of a harmful behaviour is arguably key to how you work with the young person to increase their capacity to self-care in a kinder and less harmful way.

When people hear the word 'coping', they may think of words like 'dependent', 'not in control', 'just about managing', 'passive' or 'being OK'. The term 'mood alteration' tends to evoke very different associations like 'in control', 'responsible for own choice', 'choice', 'assertive' and 'knowing what they're doing'.

Thinking about mood alteration

At the end of a busy day, do you sometimes have a glass of wine, eat some chocolate or go running? Why do you do these things? For example, for relaxation, a deserved treat/reward, to unwind, for a break between tasks, to get an emotional lift. It can be useful to think about whether you would rather be perceived as doing these things as a way to alter your mood, which you have acknowledged is the motivation for them, or doing these things to 'cope'? How you perceive this will impact how you see yourself and invite others to see you.

Reflection

Consider the differences between viewing self-injurious behaviour as a 'coping' mechanism or a 'mood alteration' so that you can improve the outcomes for young people.

When we talk about self-esteem with young people and what impacts a young person's self-esteem, we need also to examine how the views we hold about those events can either contribute negatively or positively to that young person's developing self-esteem. It is useful to have a theoretical framework to support reflections that will help us move from viewing many young people as actors in their lives rather than as being passive. The next part of this section and activity provides us with one.

It is useful to note that eating chocolate or doing a sport releases 'feel good' chemicals known as endorphins, which can also be released when a person self-injures. In the case of drinking, you have to work hard psychologically to get a lift, as alcohol is a depressant.

Important: Do not share information about self-injury and endorphins with children and young people.

23

The Transactional Analysis Drama Triangle

Transactional Analysis (TA) can be used to examine relationship dynamics. It can highlight workers' self-awareness regarding the roles and responses they may potentially occupy when working with a young person who self-injures.

The Drama Triangle illustrates how people may adopt and move between three roles. Often people will have a dominant role, which is the result of their 'script'. The 'script', also referred to as a 'life script', is an unconscious life plan *made in childhood, reinforced by parents, justified by subsequent events, and culminating in a chosen alternative'* (Berne, 1972). The Drama Triangle is useful because it can help us to make sense of our relationship with the 'self' (ourselves) and with the other (the young person

we are working with). It can also help us when we examine the impact of self-injury on us and the feelings it provokes within us and it is a useful model to make sense of how we feel and react.

The Drama Triangle shows three dominant positions: victim, persecutor and rescuer. The terms in brackets were introduced later by Acey Choy (1990) to offer a more positive use of the model – the Winner's Triangle.

For example, the word 'victim' carries more negative connotations than 'vulnerable'. Considering a young person as 'vulnerable' rather than as a 'victim' has the potential to evoke more positive reactions to your (and their) dominant stance as they are able to take responsibility for their life and develop empowering and self-nurturing strategies to support their vulnerabilities. Similarly, the

Figure 1: The Drama Triangle

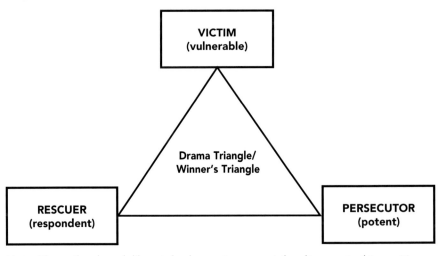

Note: The author has deliberately chosen to present the diagram in this position. Please see the explanation for this in the guidance on page 26.

Activity: What is your dominant position?

This activity aims to help you better understand the Drama Triangle dynamic and will help you to think about where you might fit on the triangle and what your dominant position is.

Read the following scenarios and consider your responses.

It's been a long day at the children's home and you've done an extra shift to cover for someone who was off sick. You're glad to get home. As soon as you get home, your phone rings. It's that friend of yours, the one who's always having some crisis or another, or yet another relationship going wrong, and they 'need' to talk to you. You, on the other hand, were looking forward to the takeaway you picked up on the way home. You're about to pour yourself a glass of wine and watch your favourite soap.

How do you respond?

1. *I carry on talking to them while putting my take away in the oven to keep warm. I say things like, 'Oh no, poor you, I know it must be hard...' An hour goes by and I'm still on the phone. I rationalise the fact my dinner is ruined on the basis that my friend can't help it and I'm glad they had me to call, but secretly I wish they'd find someone else to talk to and I'm a bit fed up that I've not had my quiet night in. (Respondent/rescuer)*

2. *I answer the phone, but I'm feeling fed up, having just muttered to the cat that it's not fair, doesn't anyone realise how hard I've worked today and there is no one here to look after me. I listen for a little while. Then I say, 'Yes I know what you mean, did I tell you I went to the doctor last week and they don't know what the matter is 'cos I keep getting headaches too, but mine have been going on since last year, and you know my mum had a brain haemorrhage, but at least she had someone to look after her'. (Vulnerable/victim)*

3. *I answer the phone and listen for a short while. I do not feel sympathetic and say things like, 'Look you've just got to get a grip, there's no point feeling down. I've told you before there's only one person you can rely on in this life, and it's yourself. Look, I've got to go, my takeaway is getting cold'. Then you flick the phone onto answer machine. (Persecutor/potent)*

word 'respondent' has more positive connotations than 'rescuer' as a respondent can provide help when the vulnerable person asks for it and this will be empowering for both the self and other as both parties are responsible for their choices and responses. For example, sometimes it is best to just sit with someone and listen to them rather than do anything.

You may notice some parallels here with the activity in which you explored words that come to mind when you think of 'coping' and 'mood alteration'.

The Drama Triangle is traditionally drawn the other way round – with the 'victim' at the bottom. In this guide it is deliberately illustrated with the 'victim/ vulnerable' or young person at the top, because those in caring professions will appropriately place the young person at the centre of care planning and at the forefront of their thinking. Due to the focus on the information received about the young person at the time of assessment, it is not surprising that the young person is often viewed and, in turn, positioned, as a 'victim'.

Metaphorically, we may place ourselves at the young person's side, hoping to help steer them on their journey. However, we need to consider what can happen within our working relationship with a young person if we position them as the 'victim' at the top of the triangle, and we also need to be mindful of the young person positioning themselves as a victim. If this dynamic occurs ie. the young person occupies the dominant

position of the 'victim', then it will follow that the professional could unwittingly be positioned and occupy either the dominant position of the persecutor or the rescuer. Good supervision and opportunities for reflective practice can support the professional in identifying these positions.

The person making the call in the scenario is occupying the dominant position of 'victim'. What can frequently happen is that despite most of us having one dominant position, we move between the other two positions dependent on the stimuli we are subjected to and/or experience. If we return to what listener one thinks towards the end of the call, we see that they start to move from rescuer to either victim or persecutor ie. '... but secretly I wish they'd find someone else to talk to, and I'm a bit fed up...'

More information would be needed to make a conclusion, but we could assume is that our reaction is informed by our 'script'.

Reflection

Despite the age of the following quote, it still reflects a common position held among many professionals: 'Of all the disturbing patient behaviours, self-mutilation is the most difficult for clinicians to understand and treat... The typical clinician (myself included) treating a patient who self-mutilates is often left feeling a combination of helpless, horrified, guilty, furious, betrayed and sad.' (Francis, 1987) It can be useful to think about how you would feel if you received this feedback from a clinician.

Would it be helpful or unhelpful?

Activity: How do you feel when you encounter self-harm?

Think about the following scenario.

You're waiting in a room to talk to a girl, aged 15, who self-injures. You have not met her before. She enters your room. She has long blonde hair and a pale complexion. She is wearing a short skirt, high UGG boots and a short-sleeved t-shirt over a long-sleeved one. At the edges of her t-shirt you can see a number of cuts and scars. None of them need immediate attention, but they clearly include recent injuries. Beneath the hem of her skirt, on her right thigh, you can see what appear to be small circular burn marks.

The voice of young people who self-injure	My feelings
Angry	
Anxious	
Concerned	
Embarrassed	
Frightened	
Frustrated	
Guilty	
Sad	
Shit	

The list on the left represents the feelings young people who self-harm have stated they feel when entering a room to see a professional/support worker.

Write down the feelings that arose in you when you read the scenario using single words.

Finally, circle any parallels between the two lists.

Professionals' reactions

In relation to the activity on page 27, many staff will include the following feelings in their list.

- Helpless
- Frustrated
- Angry
- Afraid
- Horrified
- Sad
- Furious
- Guilty
- Curious
- Concerned
- Empathy
- Embarrassed

There will be parallels between the potential feelings experienced by the professional and by the young person. The most common and parallel feelings are:

- angry
- helpless

- anxious
- worried
- concerned
- sad.

Reflect on your observations ie. the similarity between the feelings you are holding within yourself, and those held by the young people you are working with. Understanding these similarities can increase opportunities for developing successful working relationships with young people.

What do we do with these feelings?

In the previous activity, you considered how a young person and a professional may hold some of the same feelings. So what happens to these feelings?

Often the reason people self-harm is because it is a way of managing their feelings. Through self-injury they are able to 'release' the feelings and feel safe and in control. As professionals, our aim is to encourage a reduction in the young person's fear of being overwhelmed by their feelings, so that they are able to manage their feelings in a less physically harmful manner. Importantly, this can lead to the young person developing a more nurturing approach to meeting their own mental health needs.

Reflection

How do you experience working with young people who self-harm? Think about the feelings that are provoked, along with any difficulties, questions and dilemmas that you experience.

Figure 2: Potential conflict in needs and approaches

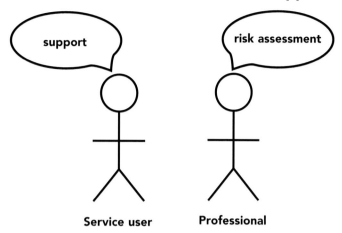

Figure 3: Closing the lid on feelings

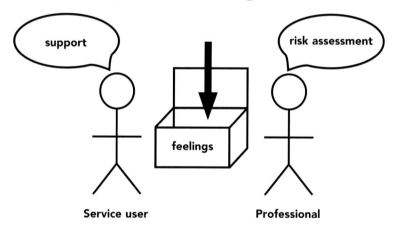

The need to complete a risk assessment is not in question. However, how staff approach its introduction to the young person is key (see Figure 2). Professionals need to remember at every opportunity that they are a role model to the young person who self-harms. Professionals can do this in an important way – by showing their own ability to manage feelings in a self-nurturing way. Many young people who self-harm have not had their feelings and/or experiences validated, therefore validating both their feelings and our own feelings when they are with us is something we all arguably need to develop skills in. It is not easy, and this is not about becoming a mini-therapist, but it is about staying 'real' in the presence of the young person. For example, if you feel uneasy or a bit unsure about self-harm – say so, don't push the feeling down.

It is very easy to put the lid down on the 'feelings' box (see Figure 3). The young person can become defensive or quiet and the professional may feel unsure and be pleased to have a form to complete because it can act as something to hide uncomfortable feelings behind. Professionals can sometimes justify the non-expression of their inner feelings (which inform and shape attitudes) to themselves and within their respective profession as a necessary way of remaining 'professional'. Yet, when working with someone who self-harms you are working with a person who has become understandably fearful of their internal world and their emotions, which can be evoked by many things, leading to the young person feeling that the only way they can contain their inner world is through self-injury.

It is important to consider ways in which professionals can refer to their own feelings that are provoked when supporting the young person and still feel professional. However, if the feeling evoked is anger then the member of staff would not be encouraged to share such feelings until they have had a supervision session. In their supervision session they would unpack what has provoked the feelings that cause them to feel anger towards the young person. For example, it may be that they have internalised what the young person is feeling. Additionally, anger is frequently an expression of fear and/or anxiety; which are both highly understandable emotions experienced in this area of work.

A history of self-mutilation

In 1938 Karl Menninger, one of America's most distinguished psychiatrists, wrote the landmark book *Man Against Himself* (1938), concluding that self-injury is about survival. Menninger had previously written a popular monthly column in 1930 in *The Ladies Home Journal* entitled 'Mental hygiene and the home'.

About self-harm behaviours, Menninger (1938) wrote: '*A recognition towards self-destructiveness is examined as a misdirection of the instinct for survival*'.

Humanity has a long history of acts of self-mutilation.

Tantum and Whittaker's (1992) article 'Personality disorder and self-wounding' introduces the prevalence of self-wounding cultures around the world and the role of religion in such acts. It refers to Karl Menninger's 1935 article 'A psychoanalytic study of the significance of self-mutilations' in *Psychoanalytic Quarterly* **4** 408–466, in which he details the religiously motivated self-wounding in cultures throughout the world. In particular, Menninger references the Tongans, Chinese thigh-cutters, indigenous peoples of South America, Bengalis, and a Russian sect of Castrati – the Skoptsi.

Historically, there are also themes of self-punishment and atonement for aggressive, destructive impulses.

Examples of historical self-mutilation

The Skoptsi, Russia: Members of this secret sect, which was founded in the late 18th century, believed that after Adam and Eve were expelled from the Garden of Eden the halves of the forbidden fruit they had eaten were grafted onto their bodies forming testicles and breasts. Skoptsi, meaning 'castrated one', lived up to their name by castrating themselves. Men's testicles and/or penises and women's breasts and labia were removed in the belief that castration would restore them to the pristine state before Adam and Eve's sin.

Tonga islanders: Curr (1887) observed the tradition of cutting part of the little finger off as a sacrifice to the gods for the recovery of a sick relative.

Self-harm also expresses:

- the will to live
- a partial or local destruction serves the purpose of gratifying urges
- meeting psychological needs
- where a person's reality sense is diminished, which can lead to self-destruction
- life instinct vs. death instinct
- a way of validating a reality.

Facts and figures about self-harm

Truth Hurts: Report of the National Inquiry into self-harm among young people (MHF, 2006) was conducted by the National Inquiry and aimed to increase understanding of self-harm. It led to changes in the prevention of, and response to, self-harm among young people in the UK. Table 1 shows some findings from the report that summarise the voice of staff and the voice of young people.

How common is self-harm?

- Between one in 12 and one in 15 young people self-harm (MHF, 2006).
- 25,000 young people present to hospitals each year with injuries as a result of self-harm (Fox & Hawton, 2004).
- Many report previous episodes when they did not go to hospital. (Fox & Hawton, 2004).
- Between 1989 and 1992 the rates of self-harm in the UK were among the highest in Europe (Fox & Hawton, 2004).

Rates of self-harming

- Highest rate of self-harm was found among 13 to 15-year-old girls (Green *et al*, 2005).
- Rates in young women (15 to 19 year olds) noted to rise since 1980s (Hawton *et al*, 2012a).
- Hawton *et al* also found a marked rise in the number of young men self-harming (Hawton *et al*, 2012a).

Table 1: The voice of staff and young people (MHF, 2006)

The voice of staff	The voice of young people
Many professionals are unaware of the extent of the problem or how best to respond	Young people who self-harm rarely asked for help directly
For many, self-harm generates a powerful emotional response	They tended to talk to friends about their problems as they experienced unhelpful responses from adults
Training about self-harm and mental health is generally very patchy	They needed to talk to someone who didn't over-react and knew how to help
Support and supervision are often inadequate	Self-harm was not talked about in schools
Information and help with self-harm is difficult to access	Young people want professionals to be honest if they do not understand
	They don't like to be called 'self-harmers'

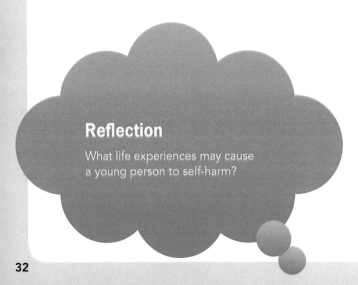

Reflection

What life experiences may cause a young person to self-harm?

Life experiences and personal characteristics associated with self-harm

A study by Hawton *et al* (2002) found that 10–12% of boys who experienced physical or sexual abuse self-harmed. A survey by Arnold (1995) found that around half of women who have experienced sexual abuse self-injure.

Young prisoners represent the largest group of individuals 'at risk' of suicide, particularly those under 21 who make up a larger remand population (Duffy & Ryan, 2004).

Family adversity factors include:

- parental separation
- parental death
- parental disorder
- a family of suicidal behaviour
- marital and family discord.

(Hawton *et al*, 2012b)

Other factors associated with self-harm include:

- depression
- having a family member or close friend who has attempted suicide or self-harmed
- low self-image and low self-esteem
- smoking (tobacco)
- drug misuse
- worries about sexual orientation
- high impulsivity
- high anxiety levels
- bullying
- poor peer/family relationships.

Relationship between ethnicity and the incidence of self-harm

Research into suicidal behaviour in ethnic groups is sparse and conflicting. Self-harm is less common in Asian young women aged 15–16 years than in white young women (Hawton *et al*, 2002). However, Asian women aged 15–35 years have been found to be 'two-to-three times more vulnerable to self-harm than their non-Asian counterparts' (EACH, 2009).

The relationship between suicide and self-harm

Professionals, including many mental health professionals, often confuse self-harm with suicide attempts and some use the terms interchangeably and wrongly (Favazza & Rosental, 1993). Self-harm, as a diagnostic feature, is without the direct intent to end life (Nock *et al*, 2006). However, people who self-harm are statistically

Reflection

Do you think there is a link between ethnicity and the incidence of self-harm?

more likely to go on to kill themselves by suicide. Also, they are more at risk from accidental death following an episode of self-harm (Royal College of Psychiatrists, 2010).

It is estimated that there are approximately 19,000 suicide attempts by adolescents every year in the UK. This equals more than one every 30 minutes (ChildLine, 2002). Attempted suicide among young women and young men increased during the 1990s (Beautrais, 2003).

Research by Mind (2010) suggests that 10% of 15 to 16 year olds have self-harmed, usually by cutting themselves, and that girls are far more likely to self-harm than boys. However, presentations at hospitals may be wrongly recorded as a suicide attempt.

In 2009, 332 men and 84 women aged 15–24 completed suicide (World Health Organization, 2012).

Young men are more at risk from accidental death due to high lethality attempts (Hawton, 2003).

Approximately 60% of persons who die as a result of suicide have a history of self-harm, with 25% of persons estimated to have previously been in contact with secondary care services as a result of their self-harm (National Institute for Mental Health in England, 2008).

Substance abuse is thought to be a highly significant factor in young men's suicide (US Department of Health and Human Services, Office of the Surgeon General and National Action Alliance for Suicide Prevention, 2012). American research has shown that one in three young men who attempt suicide were intoxicated at the time (Nemtsov, 2003).

Reflection

What harm minimisation techniques are you aware of? What drawbacks does each one have?

Harm minimisation techniques

Harm minimisation techniques that are commonly recommended include the young person using an elastic band, a red pen or ice cubes when they feel the need to self-harm. There may be drawbacks to these different harm minimisation techniques. For example, a young person may not have access to a freezer and ice cubes will melt so they are not very practical in situations where the young person is away from the home.

It is important to discuss harm minimisation techniques with the young person so that they know what can be used, as well as how they can be used. For example, if you suggest to a young person that they use a red pen to draw on themselves when they feel the need to self-harm, it is important that you explain that the pen should have a soft tip so they do not injure themselves. This is very important as there have been cases where children and young people have got septicaemia from a wound caused by a pen. Also note that using a red pen will only be useful to those who want to see the colour of blood, as for some this will hold little or no relevance.

For more information about harm minimisation techniques, see www.facebook.com/impactwellbeing

NICE self-harm guidelines

The NICE guidelines – *Self-harm: Longer-term management* (CG 133) were issued in November 2011 and followed on from *Self-harm: The short-term physical and psychological management and secondary prevention of self-harm in primary and secondary care* (NICE Clinical Guideline 16) (2004), which covered the treatment of self-harm within the first 48 hours of an incident. The 2011 guidelines are concerned with the longer-term psychological treatment and management of both single and recurrent episodes of self-harm and address service users and health and social care professionals.

The introduction recognises that self-harm is very common in young people and the guidelines are relevant to all people aged eight and older. Where

Important:
For this part of Section 1, you will need a copy of NICE Guidelines (2011) *Self-harm: Longer term management* (Clinical Guideline 133) available from: http:// guidance.nice.org.uk/CG133.

children and young people are referred to, it includes children from the ages of eight to 17. Self-harm is used to refer to any act of self-poisoning or self-injury carried out by an individual irrespective of motivation. This commonly involves self-poisoning with medication or self-injury by cutting, but does not include harm arising from excessive consumption of alcohol or recreational drugs, or from starvation arising from anorexia nervosa.

The 2011 guidelines took over five years to agree. There were significant changes between the 2004 version and the 2011 version. The most significant development being the removal of the word 'deliberate' in front of self-harm ie. we never say 'deliberate' substance misuse, 'deliberate' sexual risk taking behaviours etc. Equally significant is the emphasis for social care and health to work together and to move away from pathologising the person who self-harms. All recommended models must also be underpinned with a person-centred care approach.

The following is a summary of key areas and recommendations included in the guidelines, as a series of bulleted lists and commentary.

Prevalence of self-harm

- Young people aged 15–16 years: 10% girls and 3% boys.
- All age groups: annual prevalence approximately 0.5%.
- Increases likelihood of person dying by suicide by 50–100-fold above rest of population in a 12-month period.
- A wide range of psychiatric problems are associated with self-harm.

Assessment and risk assessment

Assessment of needs will include:

- skills, strengths and assets
- coping strategies
- mental health problems or disorders
- physical health problems or disorders
- social circumstances and problems
- psychosocial and occupational functioning and vulnerabilities
- need for psychological intervention, social care, drug treatment for assessing conditions
- the needs of any dependent children.

A risk assessment with the young person will cover:

- methods and frequency of self-harm – current and past

- current and past suicidal intent
- depressive symptoms and their relationship to self-harm
- any psychiatric illness and its relationship to self-harm
- personal, social specific factors preceding
- alternative strategies used
- significant supportive and non-supportive relationships
- immediate and longer-term risks.

It is important to ask the young person what chat rooms and internet sites they have accessed. (It's useful to familiarise yourself with those sites, recognising that they may be distressing.)

The guidelines include the importance of exploring the meaning of self-harm; since each person self-harms for individual reasons and a person's reasons can vary from episode to episode, each episode of self-harm needs to be treated in its own right.

Risk assessment tools and scales (CG 133)

The guidelines guard against the use of risk assessment tools and scales to predict future suicide or repetition of self-harm. They should not be used to determine who should and should not be offered treatment or discharged.

Care plans – short and long term

Discuss, agree and document aims. Review.

- Prevent escalation of self-harm
- Reduce harm or stop
- Reduce or stop other risk taking behaviour
- Improve social or occupational functioning
- Improve quality of life
- Improve any associated mental health conditions

Risk management plans

- A clearly identifiable part of the care plan
- Inform limits of confidentiality
- Address each long-term/immediate risk
- Identified associated factors will increase risk
- Have a crisis plan – outline self-management strategies and how to access services
- Ensure consistency between risk management plan and long-term treatment strategy

In developing integrated care and risk management plans, there is a need to:

- summarise key needs and risks
- complete this work with the service user
- complete this work with others if agreed by service user
- provide printed copies for all
- if there is disagreement, offer the opportunity for the service user to write these in their notes.

Provision of information should include the following:

- offer relevant written and verbal information about the dangers and long-term outcomes of available interventions and possible strategies
- treatment of any associated mental health conditions
- access to Understanding NICE guidance booklet (available at: http://www.nice.org.uk/nicemedia/live/13619/57175/57175.pdf)
- NICE Guideline 16.

Confidentiality and consent

- Professionals trained to understand and apply Mental Capacity Act (2005) and Mental Health Act (1983; amended 1995 & 2007)
- Familiar with principles
- Offer full written and verbal information about treatment options
- Ensure person is able to give informed consent

- Recognise capacity can rapidly change
- Easy access to legal advice

Safeguarding

- CAMHS professionals consider whether child's needs to be assessed within local safeguarding procedures
- If referred to CAMHS under local safeguarding procedures:
  1. use multidisciplinary approach
  2. consider use of Common Assessment Framework
  3. develop child protection plan if there are serious concerns
  4. consider risk of domestic violence or exploitation.

Families, carers and significant others

- Ask the person who self-harms whether they would like their family, carer, significant other to be involved
- Balance developing autonomy of child with perceived risks and responsibilities and views of carers
- Offer written and verbal information on how they can be supportive
- Offer contact numbers and what to do if there is a crisis

- Info about family and carer support groups
- Inform of their right for a formal carers assessment and how to access one

Managing endings and supporting transitions

- Anticipate endings provoking strong emotions
- Plan in advance
- Have clear contingency plans in case of crisis
- Record plans
- Give copies to service user and others
- CAMHS and AMH work collaboratively
- Time the transfer to suit person
- Continue CAMHS post-18 if realistic
- Develop local transition protocols

Referrals

Referrals are a priority when:

- levels of distress are rising, high and sustained
- risk of self-harm increasing and unresponsive to attempts to help
- the person requests help from specialist services
- levels of distress in carers rising, high or sustained despite attempts to help
- primary and secondary care to work collaboratively sharing information
- primary care to monitor physical health needs.

Harm reduction

If stopping is unrealistic in the short-term:

- consider harm reduction strategies
- reinforce existing coping strategies
- discuss less destructive or harmful methods with service users, carers etc.
- advise the service user there is no safe way to self-poison.

What do the guidelines say about the support professionals need?

- Professionals to be trained in assessment, treatment and management.
- Professionals to be educated about the stigma and discrimination usually associated with self-harm.
- Staff should be offered consultation, supervision and support.

- Involve people who self-harm in the design and delivery of training.
- Training should aim to improve the quality and experience of care.
- The effectiveness of the training needs to be assessed.
- Consideration of emotional impact of self-harm on the professional and capacity to practice competently and empathically.

Research recommendations

- Does the training improve outcomes?
- Develop a randomised controlled trial
- Include professionals and service users
- Include longer term follow up of 12 months or more
- Consider impact on service users experience and outcomes

- Effectiveness of psychosocial assessments
- Clinical and cost effectiveness
- Observational study exploring harm-reduction approaches

Reflective practice questions

Reflect on Section 1 and the issues it has raised for you on both personal and professional levels.
- What are the key learning points for you?
- What aspects of your learning will you take into your practice?
- What needs for continuing professional development have you identified?

References

Arnold L (1995) *Women and Self-injury: A survey of 76 women*. Bristol: Bristol Crisis Service for Women.

Beautrais A (2003) Suicide and serious suicide attempts in youth: a multiple group comparison study. *American Journal of Psychiatry* **160** 1093–1099.

Berne E (1972) *What Do You Say After You Say Hello? The psychology of human destiny*. New York: Grove Press.

ChildLine (2002) *ChildLine Information Sheet* **6**. London: ChildLine.

Choy A (1990) The winner's triangle. *Transactional Analysis Journal* **20** (1) 40–46.

Curr E (1887) The Australian race: its origin, languages, customs, place of landing in Australia and the routes by which it spread itself over the continent. Volume 3.

Duffy D & Ryan T (2004) *New Approaches to Preventing Suicide: A manual for practitioners*. London: Jessica Kingsley Publishers.

EACH (2009) *Asian Women, Domestic Violence and Mental Health: A toolkit for health professionals*. London: DH.

Favazza AR & Rosental (1993) Diagnostic issues in self-mutilation. *Hospital & Community Psychiatry* **44** (2) 134–140.

Francis A (1987) The borderline self-mutilator: introduction. *Journal of Personality Disorders* **1** 316.

Fox C & Hawton K (2004) *Deliberate Self-harm in Adolescence*. London: Jessica Kingsley Publishers.

Green H, McGinnity A, Meltzer H, Ford T & Goodman R (2005) *Mental Health of Children and Young People in Great Britain 2004*. London: Palgrave.

Hawkton K (2003) Deliberate self-harm in adolescents: a study characteristics and trends 1990–2000. *Journal Child Psychology and Psychiatry* **44** 119–198.

Hawton K, Rodham K, Evans, E & Weatherall R (2002) Deliberate self-harm in adolescents: self-report survey in schools in England. *British Medical Journal* **325** 1207–1211.

Hawton K, Saunders K & O'Connor R (2012a) *The Lancet* **379** (9834) 2373–2382.

Hawton K, Saunders K & O'Connor R (2012b) Self-harm and suicide in adolescence. *The Lancet* **379** (9834) 2373–2382.

Menninger K (1938) *Man Against Himself*. New York: Harcourt.

Mental Health Foundation (2006) *Truth Hurts: National Inquiry consultation into self-harm among young people*. London: MHF.

Mind (2010) *Understanding self-harm* [online]. Available at: www.mind.org.uk/help/diagnoses_and_conditions/self-harm (accessed February 2013).

National Institute for Mental Health in England (2008) *Suicide Prevention: Annual Report 2007*. Leeds: Department of Health.

Nemtsov A (2003) Suicides and alcohol consumption. *Drug and Alcohol Dependence* **71** 161–8.

NICE (2004) *Quick Reference Guide: Self-harm – The short-term physical and psychological management and secondary prevention of self-harm in primary and secondary care*. London: NICE.

NICE (2011) *Guidelines Self-harm: Longer term management* (Clinical Guideline 133). London: NICE.

Nock M, Joiner T, Gordon K, Lloyd-Richardson E & Prinstein M (2006) Non-suicidal self-injury among adolescents: diagnostic correlates and relation to suicide attempts. *Psychiatry Research* **144** 66–72.

Oppenheim AN (2000) *Questionnaire Design, Interviewing and Attitude Measurement.* London: Continuum.

Royal College of Psychiatrists (2010) *Self-harm, Suicide and Risk: Helping people who self-harm. Final report of a working group.* College Report CR158. London: RCPSYCH.

Tantum D & Whittaker J (1992) Personality disorder and self-wounding. *British Journal of Psychiatry* **161** 451–464.

US Department of Health and Human Services, Office of the Surgeon General and National Action Alliance for Suicide Prevention (2012) *National Strategy for Suicide Prevention: Goals and objectives for action.* Washington, DC: HHS.

World Health Organization (2012) *Number of Suicides by Age Group and Gender: United Kingdom of Great Britain and Northern Ireland 2009.* Available at: http://www.who.int/mental_health/media/unitkingd.pdf (accessed January 2015).

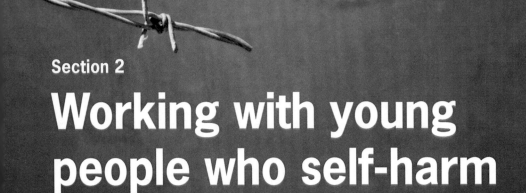

Working with young people who self-harm

Introduction

This section revisits why young people might self-harm and explores myths and fantasies about why they might engage in such behaviours. It considers what a therapeutic alliance looks like and why it is important, and it examines strategies that can promote good mental health and may support a reduction in self-injuring behaviours.

Why do people self-harm?

The importance of cultivating an enquiring mind and undertaking self-reflection cannot be overemphasised since this is where the power of learning takes place, transforming information into action learning.

Reflection

Based on your learning and reflection so far, why do you think people self-harm? You may wish to ask others for their thoughts to compare them with yours.

Activity: Self-harm 'role play'

The aim of this activity is to 'get into the skin' of a person who self-harms. Choose one of the following characters:

- *a 20-year-old woman who hears voices telling her to cut herself*
- *an 18-year-old young man who sets fire to his trousers when skateboarding*
- *a 24-year-old woman who puts bleach in her cuts.*

Take two to three minutes to make up a back story detailing a rationale for your chosen character's self-harming behaviour. Get into the character's role and write or record this rationale, as if you were explaining it to someone else.

Then 'de-role' by saying aloud your name, profession, where you work and why you are working through this guide. Look through what you have written or listen to what you have recorded.

- *How does it inform a definition of self-harm?*
- *Are there differences between definitions by a professional and by a service user?*

Self-harm 'role play'

As a result of the role play activity, you may have come to some of the following conclusions:

- Definitions differ; those completed when in character are frequently more personal and there is less use of medical language. This is in contrast to the more objective language used by professionals.
- The need to see service users as individuals becomes clearer.
- Those readers who took the role of the male service user may assume that the act of self-harm was done to impress and/or was part of male peer group activity when in fact it could have been done in isolation. This encourages participants to challenge their assumptions about a person who self-harms.
- Some readers will share the experience of not being able to communicate their character's feelings verbally.
- The use of the body as an external landscape and the way in which people care for bodies, or not, can be statements about their internal landscape.
- The importance of not focusing continually on the act of self-injury when developing a relationship with a young person who self-harms. This can lead to the worker colluding with the way the young person remains invisible ie. they and others focus on the young person's external landscape. There is an opportunity to make some parallels to working with people with eating disorders.

(A useful reference here is *Internal Landscapes and Foreign Bodies: Eating disorders and other pathologies* (Williams, 2002)).

Finally, consider the National Institute of Health and Care Excellence (2011) definition of self-harm: 'Any act of self-poisoning with medication or self-injury by cutting'.

Listening to young people's experiences

Watch the 15-minute film Sh! which is included on the enclosed DVD. Consider each young person's story and complete each column of the table, as shown in the example.

Common points raised in undertaking this activity include:

- An acknowledgement that some young people do not know why they started self-harming. Part of the focus of an assessment could be to engage the child in a conversation about the reasons why they self-harm.
- Staying with the young person's pace of change can be frustrating, so what support do staff need?
- In the film, the young person's experience of A & E is positive, however this is frequently not the case for many young people. It can raise complex issues for a nurse to support a person who chooses to injure and this can, for some, fuel anger towards the young person.
- The use of razor blades and other cutting implements is raised and how taking these away can increase

Activity: Sh! Young people's stories

Triggers	Action taken	Type of self-harm	Function/ purpose	What responses were not helpful?	What responses were helpful?
Forced sexual encounter	School nurse reference	Cut fingers/ arms	To make them feel better	Patronised	Positive treatment at A & E

the young person's feelings of distress and, in turn, increase the need to self-injure, yet we need to ensure we keep the child safe, so how do we achieve our safeguarding obligation?

- When working with a young person who does not and cannot stop self-harming, does this have an impact on how the worker takes care of themselves and the feelings that are provoked in them? (This links back to Section 1.)

- Self-harming is not about attention seeking, or is it? At this point, it is important to point out that we all seek attention from the moment we get up regarding our choices in clothing, shoes, where we socialise etc. If a young person chooses to show the marks, scars, cuts on their body this will bring attention, as within our society such marks are not condoned, but this does not mean the young person deserves any less attention than the young person who does not harm themselves in that way.

- The main challenge for the support worker is not be encouraged by the young person to be continually drawn back to focusing the conversation on self-injury. The function of self-harm is not only a way of managing the person's feelings, but frequently of keeping an emotional distance from others.

The function of self-harm

The purpose of this sub-section is to explore the function self-harm may serve in someone's life and increase

A note from the author

When I am training I have been known to walk around the room dragging an empty chair. I ask participants what they see and what, if I had arrived this morning and had been pulling the chair around beside me all day, would they be tempted to focus upon? More often than not, they answer: the chair. Working with someone who self-harms can be one of the most difficult things a practitioner can do, as the invitation by the young person, in their need to protect themselves, is to encourage them to focus on the chair. This is because, despite some of the negative and dysfunctional outcomes of living with self-harm, it also serves the young person well. So why would they not bring the chair into the room?

professionals' understanding of its potential function and their responses to it. What might hinder and what might be helpful? Professionals may assume that they have the answers to these questions, but they frequently and inadvertently make assumptions. The reflection questions on page 47 may help you to step back and consider your own experiences, as well as focus on the task of supporting a young person.

Look at the boxed summary about myths and fantasies about self-injury and as you do, consider the impact of myths and fantasies about self-injury on the therapeutic alliance.

Reflective questions

Revisit your learning from Section 1:
- What does self-harm/injury invite you to focus upon in our work/support with an individual?
- What function can this serve to the young person who self-harms?
- What function can it serve for you?

Myths and fantasies about self-injury

Arnold (1995) prompts us to dispel the following common myths, which are unhelpful beliefs when providing care for people who self-injure as they mediate against the development and maintenance of a therapeutic alliance. This means examining the importance of staff taking time out before and after they meet with a young person to examine and reflect on the emotions that are provoked in them. Participants may understand that this is good practice, but may not have explicit routines for reflection after contact with a young person. Self-harm can provoke strong emotional responses from staff and some of these can be fuelled by the myths and fantasies they hold. Many such myths and fantasies are present within the environments that staff work and live in (the language used by work colleagues, such as 'cutters', 'bingers' and 'attention seekers'), so although attending training courses can raise staff awareness, it can be difficult not to be influenced by the more common judgements and assertions made by mainstream working and living environments.

- Self-injury is a sign of madness or deep mental disturbance.
- People who self-injure are trying to kill themselves.
- People who injure themselves are a danger to others.
- Self-injury is about 'attention seeking'.
- Self-injury is used to manipulate others.
- Self-injury is just a habit to be stopped.
- People who self-injure enjoy or do not feel physical pain.

(Arnold,1995)

Below is a list of possible meanings and functions of self-injury for young people.

- A response to sexual/physical abuse
- To feel real
- High levels of dissociation
- Connect back to here and now
- Surviving
- Cope with and find relief from unbearable feelings eg. rage, guilt, frustration or anxiety
- Means of self-punishment
- Physical scars enable person to show internal scars
- Endorphin release
- Increased experience of parental deprivation

An article by Hadfield *et al* (2009) – 'Analysis of accident and emergency doctors' responses to treating people who self-harm' – explores how doctors working in A & E responded when treating people who were admitted with self-harm injuries. The main themes of the article are treating the body, silencing the self, and mirroring cultural and societal responses to self-harm. The article identifies helpful and unhelpful aspects of relationships between people who self-harm and the A & E doctors who treated them. The authors consider the clinical implications of these findings within the context of A & E doctors having limited opportunities to address the relational nature of the care they offer to this group.

Assessments and the therapeutic alliance

Assessments should be completed regarding **need** and **risk**.

Important points to practice include the following:

- consider the full list of functions of self-harm
- there is always a need to check whether judgements are informed by myth or fact
- remember to gather information and make recommendations with the young person.

Routinely revisiting the purpose of the assessment is part of the process. Here is a checklist of questions to help clarify what you are assessing with the client.

- Is it about risk of suicide?
- Is it about function of self-injury?
- Is it the impact on the person's capacity to form relationships, and the type of relationships they want?
- Is it about immediate risk of harm?
- Is it about your own needs?
- Is it about where the client places us?

Each time you meet with a young person you are reassessing what you as a professional need to assess and what both you and the young person need to complete the assessment ie. sharing your view with the young person. The professional's understanding and capacity to develop a therapeutic alliance is crucial.

The service user and the professional's working relationship is complex because there is a third party – they both have a relationship with self-harm.

However, the service user remains at the centre of decision making and person-centred care is at the heart of the assessment process (NICE, 2011).

Maintaining your sense of self during an assessment requires the practitioner to have the following skills:

- interpersonal
- listening
- questioning
- observation.

There can be an invitation to join in a relationship with self-injury rather than with the individual.

Reflection

Consider the complexity of completing an assessment in a person-centred way when some young people do not want to be engaged. What issues might need to be addressed?

Activity: Therapeutic alliance

Read the following text adapted from Burke et al (2008). Research shows that what people who self-injure find most helpful is a relationship in which they are listened to and supported, not judged, where boundaries are clear and the relationship can support them over a long period (Arnold, 1995; Connors, 1996a/1996b; Warm et al, 2002).

- *The challenge for staff is to be a friendly professional and not a professional friend.*

- *The task in establishing and maintaining a helpful therapeutic alliance with a person who self-injures is to ensure that staff remain mindful and aware of their own emotional and intellectual responses. This will guard against the possibility of professionals inadvertently repeating earlier abusive relationships and experiences.*

- *It is imperative that when life appears incredibly bleak for the person who self-injures, professional carers remain hopeful and sustained by therapeutic optimism.*

See also Managing Self-harm in Young People (2014) available at: http://www.rcpsych.ac.uk/files/pdfversion/CR192.pdf

Discuss with a colleague what a therapeutic alliance offers both a professional and their client.

General interventions when supporting a young person who self-harms

In considering general interventions when supporting a young person who self-harms, you may wish to revisit NICE guidance regarding risk assessments on page 37, as well as facts and figures about self-harm on page 31.

Sensitive wound care

Individuals should be dealt with compassionately and their level of distress should be taken into account. Injuries should be dealt with swiftly and delays in treatment should be avoided. Treatment methods should be discussed with the individual. Further information is available from NICE's *Self-harm: The short-term physical and psychological management and secondary prevention of self-harm in primary and secondary care* (NICE, 2004). (You may wish to return to the findings in the article on A & E on page 48.)

The Recovery Approach

In 2005 the National Institute for Mental Health in England recommended that

Activity: Thinking about interventions

Write down what you know and have used in relation to the following interventions:

- *Sensitive wound care*

- *Recovery approach*

- *Therapeutic relationships*

- *Developing alternatives*

all interventions for self-injury should be informed by the Recovery Approach.

The Recovery Approach has 12 guiding principles.

1. The user of services decides if and when to begin the recovery process.
2. All services must be aware of the risk of service user dependency.
3. Users of services are able to recover more quickly when their:
   - hope is encouraged
   - life roles with respect to work and meaningful activities are defined
   - spirituality is considered
   - culture is understood
   - educational needs are identified
   - socialisation needs are identified
   - they are supported to achieve their goals.
4. Individual differences are considered and valued across the lifespan.
5. Recovery is more effective when a holistic approach is considered.
6. In order to reflect current best practices there is a need for an integrated approach to treatment and care that includes medical, biological, psychological, social values based and recovery approaches.
7. There needs to be an initial emphasis on hope and the ability to develop trusting relationships.
8. Care should operate from a strengths and assets model.
9. Service users should collaboratively develop recovery management or wellness recovery action plans.
10. The involvement of a person's family, partners and friends may enhance the recovery process.
11. Mental health services (equally applicable to children's services) are most effective when delivery is within the context of service users locality and cultural context.
12. Community involvement as defined by the user of service is central to the recovery process.

(NIMHE, 2005)

These principles are very useful to share when working with a young person. They were designed with adult mental health service users in mind; however they can be equally useful when working with a young person. They can be used to develop a contract which will support the therapeutic alliance that a professional and the young person are seeking to achieve.

Therapeutic relationships

Arnold (1995) talks of the importance of therapeutic relationships throughout her work. She argues that it is a relationship that offers containment for a person's anxiety and mental distress. The containment in turn offers a place for the person who self-injures to recover.

The following quotes are from research carried out in primary care, although they are relevant to work with young people who self-injure, who are frequently in contact with services within primary care.

'Building relationships is central to nursing work and communication skills can be improved by avoiding jargon and ensuring patients are not labelled' (Collins, 2009).

Good communication helps to build a therapeutic relationship.

'…More recently, a leading primary care academic has presented evidence, drawing on some 50 primary studies and systematic reviews, that a good-quality therapeutic relationship (mostly measured in terms of the popular construct 'patient-centredness') improves patient satisfaction and professional fulfilment, saves time, increases compliance with prescribed medication, and greatly reduces the chance of the practitioner being sued (Stewart, 2005 in Greenhalgh & Heath, 2010)

The latter part of this quote could be viewed as contentious, but there is a reality that workers need to offer services which enhance the quality of the work for both the service user's experience as well as the worker.

Greenhalgh & Heath (2010) conclude:

'In summary, the socio-technical dimension of the therapeutic relationship – in other words, the extent to which it follows the 'logic of care' – might be addressed via the three questions, for the purposes of this exercise the questions have been adapted to support our work with young people who self-harm, to help a worker in their own work to review the function and role they are serving in their relationship with the young person:

To what extent is the clinical relationship continuous, adaptive and sensitive to the nature and context of the self-harm?

To what extent does the clinician acknowledge, understand and seek to optimise the patient's position within a wider socio-technical care network?

To what extent is the network of therapeutic relationships supporting the service user stable and mutually adaptive as opposed to unstable and conflict-ridden?'

Developing alternatives

This refers to harm minimisation, the use of diaries and the self-harm vs. self-nurturing scales tool etc. In supporting a young person, you will need to ensure that the use of any alternative is written into the young person's care plan.

Specialist interventions when supporting a young person who self-harms

There are a number of specific therapies that are beneficial for people who self-injure and these are briefly described next. These interventions should be delivered by appropriately trained and supervised staff and research has proven that the interventions listed have long-term efficacy.

'In the majority of cases people who self-injure will have some significant personality difficulties, whether diagnosed or not, and again the research emphasises the importance of engaging in interventions into the longer term.' (Alwyn *et al*, 2006)

Psychodynamic psychotherapy

Treatment approaches that are based in the here-and-now relationship between client and therapist have been shown to be beneficial.

Mentalisation-based treatment

Mentalisation-based treatment focuses on enabling a person to understand their own thoughts and feelings and the thoughts and feelings of others.

Group therapy

Research supports the value of group psychotherapy for people who self-injure. Groups must be carefully managed to ensure that therapy does not trigger self-harm behaviours and to prevent a culture developing where self-injury equates to status.

Developmental group psychotherapy

Many young people want to belong to a group and group treatment can be a way to facilitate growth for individual members. Being part of a group may help young people to feel included and less isolated.

Dialectic behaviour therapy (DBT)

DBT is a three-stage treatment approach developed by Marsha Linehan. The first stage sees the therapist preparing for the therapeutic relationship by recognising their own prejudices and concerns which may influence treatment with a client.

The second stage sees the therapist helping the client to understand the reasons and functions of self-injury, and the third stage is about the client acquiring and practising skills such as emotional regulation.

Creative therapies

Creative therapies such as art therapy, psychodrama and dramatherapy may help a person who has difficulty articulating their feelings to access their emotions.

The following activity returns to the concept of general interventions (see page 50).

The activity on the next page raises the need to consider and take care of your own needs ie. self-care. It highlights the importance of self-care being at the forefront of your work with young people who self-harm, to encourage and not lose sight of the young person's capacity to self-care, and the need for the person offering support/ working with the young person who self-harms to also self-care.

References

Alwyn N, Blackburn R, Davidson K, Hilton M, Logan C & Shine J (2006) *Understanding Personality Disorder: A report*. London: BPS.

Arnold L (1995) *Women and Self-injury: A survey of 76 women*. Bristol: Bristol Crisis Service for Women.

Burke M, Duffy D, Trainor G & Shinnier M (2008) *Self-injury: A recovery and evidence based toolkit*. Bolton: Bolton, Stafford and Trafford Mental Health NHS Trust.

Collins S (2009) Good communication helps to build a therapeutic relationship. *Nursing Times* 19 June.

Connors R (1996a) Self-injury in trauma survivors 1: functions and meanings. *American Journal of Orthopsychiatry* **66** (2) 197–206.

Connors R (1996b) Self-injury in trauma survivors 2: levels of clinical response. *American Journal of Orthopsychiatry* **66** (2) 207–215.

Greenhalgh T & Heath I (2010) *Measuring Quality in the Therapeutic Relationship*. London: Kings Fund.

Hadfield J, Brown D, Pembroke L & Hayward M (2009) Analysis of accident and emergency doctor's responses to treating people who self-harm. *Qualitative Health Research* **19** (6) 755–765. Available at: http://qhr.sagepub.com/content/19/6/755 (accessed January 2015).

NICE (2004) Self-harm: the short-term physical and psychological management and secondary prevention of self-harm in primary and secondary care (CG16) [online]. Available at: http://www.nice.org.uk/guidance/cg16 (accessed January 2015).

NICE (2011) *Guidelines Self-harm: Longer term management (Clinical Guideline 133)* [online]. Available at: http://www.nice.org.uk/guidance/cg133 (accessed January 2015).

Reflective practice activity

Reflect on the content of Section 2 and the issues it has raised for you on both personal and professional levels.

- What are key learning points for you?
- What aspects of your learning have you (or will you) put into practice?
- What needs for continuing professional development have you identified, if any?

Activity: The self-harm and self-nurturing spectrum

Below is a list of activities/areas of life. This is a useful tool to promote conversation and learn more about the person you are working with. Try completing it yourself – remember to be honest! Score yourself between 0–20 (20 being the highest self-nurturing, 0 being the highest self-harm).

Eating   0 ←—————————→ 20

Sleeping   0 ←—————————→ 20

Working   0 ←—————————→ 20

Exercise   0 ←—————————→ 20

Leisure/relaxing   0 ←—————————→ 20

Partner/sexual relationships   0 ←—————————→ 20

Friendships   0 ←—————————→ 20

Family relationships   0 ←—————————→ 20

Alcohol/drugs   0 ←—————————→ 20

Spending   0 ←—————————→ 20

NIMHE (2005) *NIMHE Guiding Statement on Recovery* [online]. Available at: http://178.79.149.115/wp-content/uploads/2012/01/NIMHE_Guiding_Statement_on_Recovery.pdf (accessed January 2015).

Warm A, Murray C & Fox J (2002) Who Helps? Supporting people who self-harm. *Journal of Psychiatric and Mental Health* 11 (2) 121–130.

Williams G (2002) *Internal Landscapes and Foreign Bodies: Eating disorders and other pathologies.* London: Karnack.

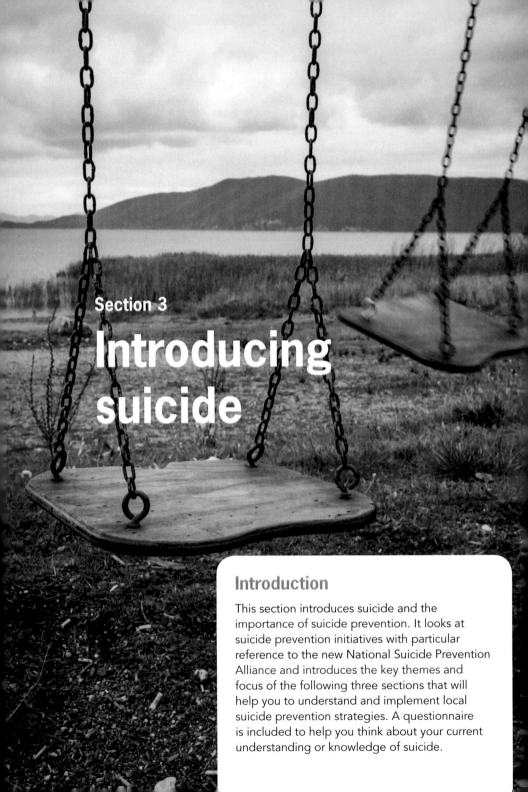

Section 3

Introducing suicide

Introduction

This section introduces suicide and the importance of suicide prevention. It looks at suicide prevention initiatives with particular reference to the new National Suicide Prevention Alliance and introduces the key themes and focus of the following three sections that will help you to understand and implement local suicide prevention strategies. A questionnaire is included to help you think about your current understanding or knowledge of suicide.

Across the world there is a growing interest in youth suicide prevention. The approaches taken vary considerably and public interest is sadly often provoked by an area or country experiencing a number of completed suicides. The US is an example of a country where increased time, research and investment in developing youth suicide prevention programmes – particularly encouraging guidance for schools – can be seen to have occurred in recent years. Similarly, this is the case in Canada and Sweden. The UK's political stance has, again, recently highlighted a commitment to reduce suicide.

In 2014, a new National Suicide Prevention Alliance (NSPA) was launched aimed at reducing the number of suicides in England and improving support for those affected by suicide.

Supported by a two-year government grant, its members include the Samaritans, Rethink Mental Illness and the Department of Health.

The core aims of the NSPA are:

- to build an active network of organisations committed to reducing suicide and supporting those affected by suicide
- to raise awareness and build knowledge of issues around suicide
- to deliver commitment and influence to suicide prevention and the National Suicide Prevention Strategy
- to mobilise action driven by shared priorities
- to share good practice

- to improve support for people at risk of suicide and for those worried about a loved one and those bereaved by suicide.

Over the next two years, the NSPA aims to provide support materials for local authorities, and establish a shared position and course of action on suicide-related websites. It will also commission a report identifying nationally available suicide prevention training and develop a national framework to support those bereaved by suicide.

The remaining three sections of this guide aim to offer the initial stepping stones to create a foundation on which a robust programme aimed at reducing suicide as a choice by young people can be created locally. They are intended to equip staff with increased knowledge, confidence, understanding and sensitivity about the subject of suicide, so staff, in turn, can support the development of local suicide prevention guidelines.

Key themes in suicide prevention will be covered:

- evidence of hope
- language of suicide
- reducing stigma
- myths and facts – introducing the notion of fearlessness
- risk vs. resilience factors
- those bereaved by suicide.

The content can be used to encourage discussion and share information, which will enable professionals and service providers to unpack some of the myths and facts surrounding the act of suicide. The author is the founder of Impact Wellbeing, a social enterprise set up to tackle the impact of trauma and build resilience in children and young people. In 2013, Impact Wellbeing produced a film accompanied by a short guide to support staff and young people to openly discuss youth suicide.

The overall aim is to 'build a suicide safer community'. This means working with and supporting children and young people in a community that demonstrates a commitment to suicide prevention, provides compassionate care and support to those bereaved by suicide, and promotes the mental health and wellness of its citizens.

The phrase 'build a suicide safer community' was coined by the Canadian Association for Suicide Prevention, which has produced a wealth of useful material on the subject.

Activity: Questionnaire

Complete the following questionnaire. It will help you to consider your own knowledge and experience of the topics that will be covered in the rest of the guide.

Do you know of any children who have stated they want to die? If so, how many?

....

How old were they?

....

What was their gender?

....

How many children up to the age of 19 years do you think are estimated to kill themselves each year in the UK?

....

How many children up to the age of 19 years in England do you think are likely to have suicidal thoughts?

....

What services are in place to support a child who contemplates suicide and/or attempts to die by suicide in your area?

....

....

....

....

Have you asked children and young people how frequently they have accessed internet sites on self-harm and suicide? If so, how many sites are you aware of?

....

....

....

What services are in place locally to support children and families following a suicide?

....

....

....

Would you know what to say to a child who wants to die?

....

....

....

What support is available to you when you are supporting a child who feels hopeless and despairing?

....

....

....

Are there local protocols in schools following a youth suicide?

....

....

....

Make a note of particular questions about the subject of suicide.

....

....

....

....

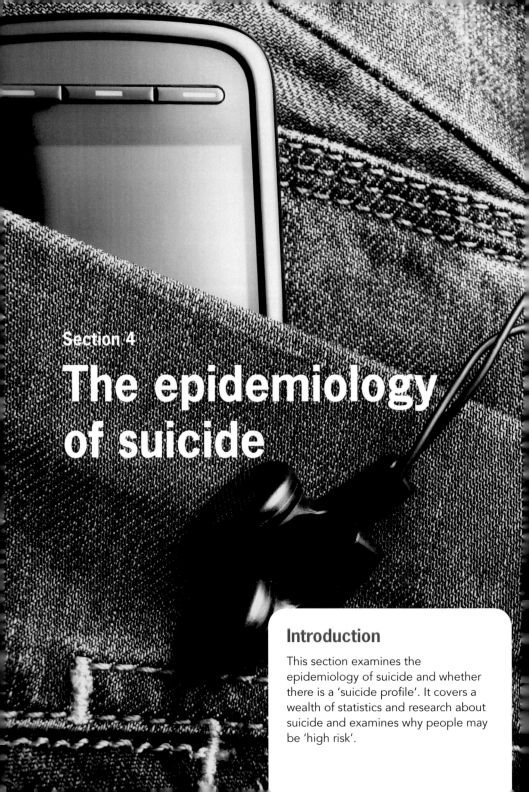

Section 4

The epidemiology of suicide

Introduction

This section examines the epidemiology of suicide and whether there is a 'suicide profile'. It covers a wealth of statistics and research about suicide and examines why people may be 'high risk'.

It is likely that in reading this guide a key question has remained in the forefront of your mind: Why do people die by suicide?

Notice that the word 'die' rather than 'commit' was used in this question. The usage of the word 'commit' will be returned to again and discussed in greater detail in Section 5.

Suicide is a complex issue involving numerous factors and it should not be attributed to a single cause. Many people who die by suicide have experienced feelings of hopelessness, helplessness and despair, and they may feel that suicide is the only way to stop their suffering. There can be many factors that can contribute to a person's decision to end their life, including relationship breakdown, addiction, bereavement, trauma, physical illness and mental illness.

Reflection

Why do you think people choose to die by suicide?

National and international suicide prevention strategies

Box 1 summarises the policies in place in different areas of the UK as well as providing some examples of international policies.

Box 1: National and international suicide prevention strategies

Wales: In 2009, the Welsh Government published *Talk to Me: The National Action Plan to Reduce Suicide and Self Harm in Wales, 2009–2014.* Available at: http://wales.gov.uk/docs/phhs/publications/talktome/091102talktomeen.pdf

Scotland: In Scotland, a 10-year Choose Life suicide prevention strategy and action plan was launched in 2002 by the Scottish Executive with the overarching aim to reduce suicide in Scotland by 20% by 2013. Available at: http://www.scotland.gov.uk/Resource/Doc/328405/0106170.pdf

Northern Ireland: In 2006, the Department of Health, Social Services and Public Safety in Northern Ireland published *Protect Life: A Shared Vision – The Northern Ireland Suicide Prevention Strategy and Action Plan, 2006–2011.* Available at: http://www.dhsspsni.gov.uk/suicide_strategy.pdf

UK: *The National Confidential Inquiry into Suicide and Homicide by People with Mental Illness – Annual Report: England, Wales, and Scotland.* Available at: http://www.bbmh.manchester.ac.uk/cmhr/centreforsuicideprevention/nci/reports/Annualreport2014.pdf

International policies: Switzerland (2005) Suizid und Suizidprävention in der Schweiz; Austria (2008) Österreichische Suizidpräventionsplan; Holland (2010) Reducing Suicidality in Netherlands

Wales

Following a public consultation in 2009, the Welsh Government published *Talk to Me: The National Action Plan to Reduce Suicide and Self Harm in Wales 2009–2014*. The action plan also highlights a Suicide Prevention Health Gain Target that has been in place since 2002 – to reduce the European age-standardised rate by 10% by 2012. Progress towards this target was reported in the Chief Medical Officer for Wales Annual Report 2010. Available at: http://wales.gov.uk/docs/phhs/publications/talktome/091102talktomeen.pdf

Scotland

In Scotland, a 10-year Choose Life suicide prevention strategy and action plan was launched in 2002 by the Scottish Executive with the overarching aim to reduce suicide in Scotland by 20% by 2013. A summary of progress to date and recommended objectives (which are similar to those in England and Wales) for the strategy were reported by the Scottish Government in 2010. Available at: http://www.isdscotland.org

Northern Ireland

In 2006, the Department of Health, Social Services and Public Safety in Northern Ireland published *Protect Life: A Shared Vision – The Northern Ireland Suicide Prevention Strategy and Action Plan, 2006–2011*. The strategy includes two targets: (i) to obtain a 10% reduction in the overall suicide rate by 2008; and (ii) to reduce the overall suicide rate by a further 5% by 2011. The latest information on suicide in Northern Ireland can be found in the *National Confidential Inquiry into Suicide and Homicide by People with Mental Illness: Annual report: England, Northern Ireland, Scotland and Wales* in July 2014. Available at: http://www.bbmh.manchester.ac.uk/cmhr/centreforsuicideprevention/nci/reports/annualreport2014.pdf

UK-wide

The National Confidential Inquiry into Suicide and Homicide by People with Mental Illness – Annual Report: England, Wales, Scotland and Northern Ireland was published in July 2014. The report provides an in-depth analysis of the changing patterns and risk factors behind cases of suicide and homicide by people in contact with mental health services along with cases of sudden unexplained death among psychiatric inpatients. Available at: http://www.bbmh.manchester.ac.uk/cmhr/centreforsuicideprevention/nci/reports/annualreport2014.pdf

Current policy in England

In *Preventing Suicide in England: A cross-government outcomes strategy to save lives* (2012), the ministerial foreword states: 'In England, one person dies every two hours as a result of suicide. When someone takes their own life, the effect on their family and friends is devastating. Many others involved in providing support and care will feel the impact.' (Department of Health, 2012)

Box 2 details those who have a role in implementation.

The Department of Health views health and well-being boards as key to the implementation of the National Suicide Strategy Implementation Advisory group's recommendations and those detailed in the Samaritans' Call to Action (2010) report. Equally importantly, work in this area will be bedded into the implementation of *No Health Without Mental Health* (HM Government, 2011) and the role of school health and mental health providers is key in preventing suicide.

The National Patient Safety Agency has produced suicide prevention toolkits for ambulance services, general practice, emergency departments and community mental health and mental health services. The toolkits support clinicians and managers to understand what they can do to reduce suicides. See: www.nhsconfed.org/Publications/briefings/Pages/Preventing-suicide.aspx

Reflection

Do you know which organisations or agencies are responsible for implementing suicide prevention strategy in your local area?

Box 2: Whose role is it?

- Local safeguarding boards
- Anti-bullying projects (see www.stonewall.org.uk/at_school/education_for_all/default.asp)
- Child and adolescent mental health services
- Health and well-being boards: see *Healthy Lives, Healthy People: Our strategy for public health in England* (2010)
- *No Health Without Mental Health: A cross government outcomes strategy for people of all ages* (HM Government, 2011) is key in supporting reductions in suicide among the general population as well as those under the care of mental health services. The first agreed objective of *No Health Without Mental Health* aims to ensure that more people will have good mental health
- Schools/education
- Primary care
- Social care
- Home Office.

The evidence base

Some of the factors when considering the evidence base for suicide include:

- reliability of statistics
- geographical variations
- information requests
- who is compiling the data?

Data may be taken from small cohorts of people and the figures relating to the actual completion of suicide are dependent upon a definition and a verdict by a coroner. Both factors can differ between countries and areas within a country.

Annually there are around 30,000 coroner's inquests held in England and Wales that conclude with a verdict (Hill & Cook, 2011). Short form verdicts cover accident or misadventure; natural causes; suicide; and homicide and make up the majority of all verdict conclusions. Narrative verdicts can be used by a coroner or jury to express conclusions about the cause of death following an inquest. In recent years there has been a large increase in the number of narrative verdicts returned by coroners in England and Wales. You can find more information to support the discussion in the articles by Gunnell (2011) and Hill & Cook (2011).

Countries handle and collect information in different ways and it is important to be mindful of this. You may want to read Daniel Rautio's article on youth and teen suicide statistics, which is available at: http://web4health.info/en/answers/bipolar-suicide-statistics.

Reflection

What might explain the results of the study in Box 4?

Box 3 shows the suicide rates in the UK between 2006–2010.

Box 3: Suicide rates in the UK between 2006–2010

In the UK, suicide is defined as deaths given an underlying cause of intentional self-harm or injury/poisoning of undetermined intent.

Key points from the statistical bulletin (ONS, 2012):

- In 2010 there were 5,608 suicides in people aged 15 years and over in the UK, 67 fewer than the 5,675 recorded in 2009.
- There were 4,231 suicides among men in 2010 (17.0 per 100,000 population).
- In women there were 1,377 suicides in 2010 (5.3 per 100,000 population).
- In 2010 suicide rates were highest in those aged 45–74 at 17.7 per 100,000 for men and 6.0 per 100,000 for women.

Table 2: Number of suicides by age group and gender in UK (2009)

Age (years)	5–14	15–24	25–34	35–44	45–54	55–64	65–74	75+	All
Males	4	332	564	830	712	457	219	195	3313
Females	3	84	133	195	191	148	81	97	932
Total	7	416	697	1025	903	605	300	292	4245

World Health Organization (2012)

Box 4 shows a study of young people in the UK and the rates of suicide between males and females. It is interesting to note that there was a 30% reduction in male suicide over the study period, but not in female suicide.

Further information about suicide rates in England and by country are outlined in the next two boxes.

Box 4: Study of 10–19 year olds in the UK

- Over a seven year period (1997–2003) the rate of suicide corresponded to an average rate of 3.28 per 100,000 per year. Note the marked gender differences (males: females = 4.79:1.69) in this age group.
- There was evidence of a 30% decline in male but not female suicides during the study period.
- The overall suicide rate for 15 to 19-year-olds was more than 12 times higher than that for 10- to 14-year-olds.

Windfuhr et al (2008)

Box 5: Suicide rates in regions in England

'Since 2000 suicide rates for males have tended to be the highest in the northern regions and lowest in the east of England and London. In 2009 rates were highest in the northwest, northeast and southwest at 19.8, 19.2 and 18.9 per 100,000 respectively. The regions with the lowest rates were London and the east of England at 13.6 and 13.7 per 100,000 respectively.'

'There was no clear pattern in regional suicide rates among women. The highest rates were dispersed over the northern and southern regions. In 2009 female rates were highest in the northwest and southwest at 5.9 and 5.7 per 100,000 respectively, and lowest in Yorkshire and the Humber, the northeast and the east of England at 3.6, 4.0 and 4.2 per 100,000 respectively.'
(ONS, 2011)

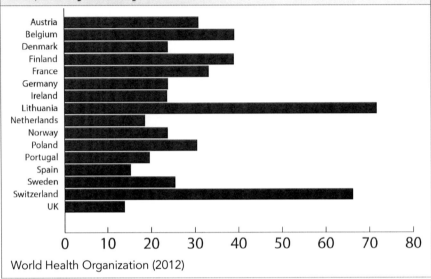

Figure 4: Average suicide rates for men and women per 100,000 by country

World Health Organization (2012)

With regard to suicide by people with mental illness, the *National Confidential Inquiry into Suicide and Homicide by People with Mental Illness* (2012) contained in the following key findings:

- The number of deaths by suicide among mental health patients treated at home was found to have reached 150–200 a year.

- There was a sustained fall in inpatient suicides across all countries.

- There was a decrease in the number of patient suicides by overdose of tricyclic antidepressants in England, Wales and Scotland.

- There were higher figures for alcohol misuse and dependence in Northern Ireland and Scotland.

- There was a rise in suicide rates in Northern Ireland, linked to alcohol misuse.

- There was a recent decrease in the number of mental health patients convicted of homicide (although it was noted to be too early to draw definitive conclusions).

- Homicides in the general population in Scotland have seen a downward trend since 2004.

(Centre for Mental Health and Risk, 2012)

The Inquiry's findings concerning the common methods of suicide by inpatients included:

- 'The most common methods of suicide by patients were hanging, self-poisoning, and jumping/multiple injuries.

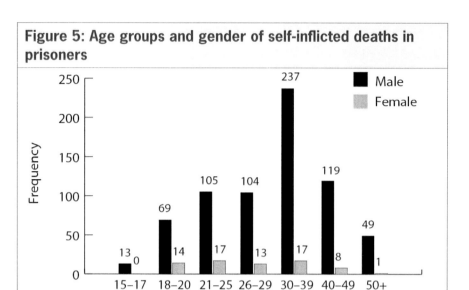

Figure 5: Age groups and gender of self-inflicted deaths in prisoners

University of Manchester (2011)

- The number of deaths by self-poisoning carbon monoxide poisoning, and drowning was found to have decreased. There was also a fall in the number of deaths by firearms (from an average of 15 deaths in 2000–2001 to five deaths in 2009–2010). Numbers remained stable for hanging, jumping/multiple injuries, and cutting/stabbing.

- The most common substances used in deaths by self-poisoning were opiates (21%), tricyclic antidepressants (16%) and paracetamol/opiate compounds (13%).

- There was a decrease of self-poisonings by tricyclic antidepressants and paracetamol/opiate compounds over the report period.'

(Centre for Mental Health and Risk, 2012)

Suicide rates among prisoners and primary psychiatric diagnosis are outlined in the next three figures.

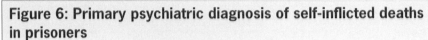

Figure 6: Primary psychiatric diagnosis of self-inflicted deaths in prisoners

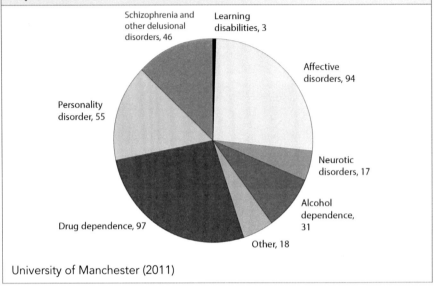

Schizophrenia and other delusional disorders, 46

Learning disabilities, 3

Affective disorders, 94

Personality disorder, 55

Neurotic disorders, 17

Alcohol dependence, 31

Drug dependence, 97

Other, 18

University of Manchester (2011)

Figure 7: Timing of self-inflicted death from reception into prison

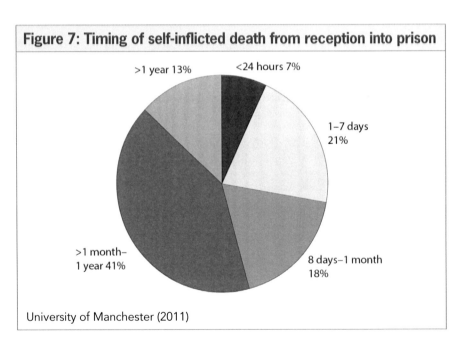

>1 year 13%

<24 hours 7%

1–7 days 21%

>1 month–1 year 41%

8 days–1 month 18%

University of Manchester (2011)

The final figure shows the main methods of suicide in the general population.

Figure 8: Suicide in the general population: main causes of death

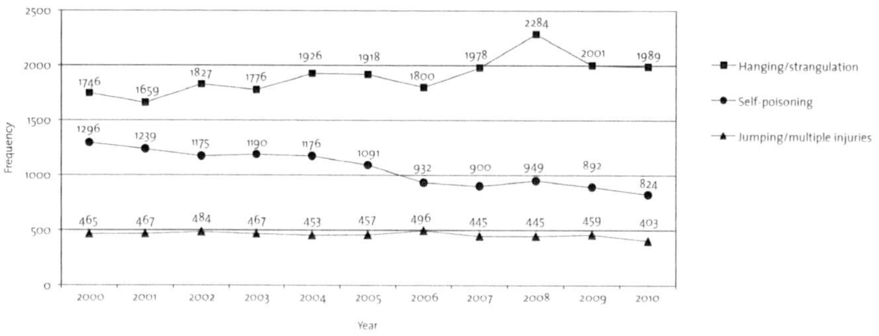

A review of the literature concerning the impact of restricting paracetamol pack size by Hawkins *et al* (2007) noted the following: 'Paracetamol (acetaminophen) is the most common drug taken in overdose in the UK, accounting for 48% of poisoning admissions to hospital and being involved in an estimated 100–200 deaths per year.'

High risk groups

The following groups could be considered at higher risk:

- people with mental illness
- people with drug and alcohol abuse
- young men are an especially vulnerable group
- people bereaved by suicide
- survivors of sexual, physical and emotional abuse
- marginalised groups and migrants

Reflection

Who might be at a greater risk of suicide?

- those in high risk occupations (farmers, nurses, doctors)
- prisoners
- unemployed people
- children and young people
- older people
- people with HIV/AIDS
- people with physical illnesses
- women during and after pregnancy.

Official policy tells us the following:

'The past couple of years have seen a slight increase in suicide rates, but the 2008–2010 rate remains one of the lowest rates in recent years. There has been a sustained reduction in the rate of suicide in young men under the age of 35, reversing the upward trend since the problem of suicides in this group first escalated over 30 years ago. We have also seen significant reductions in inpatient suicides and self-inflicted deaths in prison.' (Department of Health, 2012)

The groups at high risk of suicide are:

- young and middle-aged men
- people in the care of mental health services, including inpatients
- people with a history of self-harm
- people in contact with the criminal justice system
- specific occupational groups, such as doctors, nurses, veterinary workers, farmers and agricultural workers
- those who have been bullied or are bullying others.

The Knowsley Public Health Intelligence and Evidence team examined local data to look for patterns. The Mental Health Equity Audit (NHS, 2010) looked at the characteristics of the people who died by suicide, the frequency of methods used, contributing factors and contact with either GP or mental health services during the year before the person took their life. Their findings were based on those of the Knowsley Public Health Intelligence and Evidence team which examined local data to look for patterns and are summarised below:

Characteristics
- All white British males
- Aged 14–84 (peak 30–44)
- Over 50% unemployed

Method
- Hanging in home environment most common

Contributing factors
- Personal circumstances perceived as triggers eg. argument with partner
- 50% consumed alcohol; 33% non-prescription drugs

Contact with health services
- 33% had seen GP in last 12 months
- 33% in contact with mental health services

(NHS, 2010)

A study by Houston *et al* (2001) found the following clinical factors for suicide in young people (aged 15–24):

- mental illness
- self-harm
- drug/alcohol misuse
- personality disorder.

The following newspaper extract about early suicide attempts by David Walliams highlights the correlation between bullying and suicide and leads us into the next section, which covers the key areas to consider when thinking about youth suicide prevention.

'TV funnyman David Walliams has revealed he has tried to kill himself several times during his life-long battle with depression.

The Little Britain star said he made the first attempt when he was 12.

Writing in his autobiography, *Camp David*, he revealed he tried to hang himself the first time after he was bullied during a Sea Scouts camp.

He took an overdose when he was 19, tried to hang himself again in 2003 and cut his throat and wrists with a kitchen knife in the same year.

In a diary entry at the time, he wrote: "Earlier I had come close to stepping in front of a train. I am in total despair."

His book also reveals he spent time in The Priory being treated for depression.'

(Independent, 2012)

Reflective practice activity

Reflect on the content of Section 4 and the issues it has raised for you on both personal and professional levels.
- What are the key learning points for you?
- What aspects of your learning will you take into your practice?
- What needs for continuing professional development have you identified, if any?

References

Centre for Mental Health and Risk (2012) *The National Confidential Inquiry into Suicide and Homicide by People with Mental Illness: Annual report.* Available at: http://www.medicine.manchester.ac.uk/cmhr/centreforsuicideprevention/nci/reports/annual_report_2012.pdf (accessed January 2015).

Department of Health (2012) *Preventing suicide in England: A cross-government outcomes strategy to save lives.* London: DH. Available at: http://www.dh.gov.uk/health/files/2012/09/Preventing-Suicide-in-England-A-cross-government-outcomes-strategy-to-save-lives.pdf (accessed January 2015).

Gunnel D, Hawton K & Kapur N (2011) Coroner's verdicts and suicide statistics in England and Wales. *British Medical Journal* 343 d 6030.

Hawkins LC, Edward JN & Dargan PI (2007) Impact of restricting paracetamol pack sizes on paracetamol poisoning in the United Kingdom: a review of the literature. *Drug Safety* 30 (6) 465–476.

Hill C & Cook L (2011) Narrative verdicts and their impact on mortality statistics in England and Wales. *Health Statistics Quarterly* 49 81–100.

HM Government (2010) *Healthy Lives, Healthy People: our strategy for public health in England.* London: HM Government.

HM Government (2011) *No Health without Mental Health: A cross-government mental health outcomes strategy for people of all ages.* London: DH.

Houston K, Hawton K & Shepperd R (2001) Suicide in young people aged 15-24: a psychological autopsy study. *Journal of Affective Disorders* 63 (1–3) 159–70.

Independent (2012) David Walliams reveals suicide attempts [online]. Available at: http://www.independent.co.uk/news/people/news/david-walliams-reveals-suicide-attempts-8196829.html (accessed January 2015).

NHS (2010) *Mental Health Equity Audit* (2010). Available at: http://www.knowsley.nhs.uk/assets/uploaded/documents/KPCT2736295_mhequityauditfinalreportrevised.pdf (accessed January 2012).

Office for National Statistics (2011) *bulletin 1: Suicide rates in the United Kingdom, 2000–2009.* Available at: http://www.ons.gov.uk/ons/rel/subnational-health4/suicides-in-the-united-kingdom/2010/stb-statistical-bulletin.html (accessed January 2015).

Office for National Statistics (2012) *Statistical Bulletin: Suicide rates in the United Kingdom, 2006 to 2010* [online]. Available at: http://www.ons.gov.uk/ons/rel/subnational-health4/suicides-in-the-united-kingdom/2010/stb-statistical-bulletin.html (accessed January 2012).

Samaritans (2010) *Call to Action for Suicide Prevention in England.* Surrey: Samaritans/DH.

University of Manchester (2011) *A National Study of Self-Inflicted Deaths in Prison Custody in England and Wales from 1999 to 2007. The National Confidential Inquiry into Suicide and Homicide by People with Mental Illness.* Available at: http://www.bbmh. manchester.ac.uk/ cmhr/centreforsuicideprevention/nci/reports/ prisonsreport2011.pdf (accessed January 2015).

Welsh Assembly Government (2009) *Talk to Me: the national action plan to reduce suicide and self-harm in Wales 2009–2014.* Cardiff: WAG.

Windfuhr K, While D, Hunt I, Turnbull P, Lowe R, Burns J, Swinson N, Shaw J, Appleby L & Kapur N (2008) Suicide in juveniles and adolescents in the United Kingdom. *Journal of Child Psychology and Psychiatry* 49 (11) 1155–1165

World Health Organization (2012) *Number of Suicides by Age Group and Gender: United Kingdom of Great Britain and Northern Ireland 2009.* Available at: http://www.who.int/mental_ health/media/unitkingd.pdf (accessed January 2015).

Further reading: review articles

Mann JJ, Apter A, Bertolote J, Beautrais A, Currier D, Haas A, Hegerl U, Lonnqvist J, Malone K, Marusic A, Mehlum L, Patton G, Phillips M, Rutz W, Rihmer Z, Schmidtke A, Shaffer D, Silverman M, Takahashi Y, Varnik A, Wasserman D, Yip P & Hendin H (2005) Suicide prevention strategies: a systematic review. *JAMA* **294** (16) 2064—2074.

Rihmer Z, Kántor Z, Rihmer A & Seregi K (2004) Suicide Prevention Strategies: A brief review. *Neuropsychopharmacol Hung* **6** (4) 195—199.

Goldney RD (2005) Suicide prevention: a pragmatic review of recent studies. *Crisis* **26** (3) 128—140.

Leitner M, Barr W & Hobby L (2008) *Effectiveness of Interventions to Prevent Suicide and Suicidal Behaviour: A systematic review.* Edinburgh: The Scottish Government.

Key areas in youth suicide prevention

Introduction

This section offers the opportunity to gain an understanding of the role of hope and the lack of hope that may be experienced by vulnerable young people. It also explores the language of suicide and how it is unhelpful to use the term 'commit' to describe suicide. By highlighting and examining common myths, including the notion that individuals are 'cowards', it also addresses the stigma surrounding suicide and the need to reduce it in order to reach and connect with young people experiencing suicidal thoughts and feelings.

Hope is arguably an illusive, although an important concept. We each hold our own definition of what it means. When we struggle with loss, uncertainty, fear and sadness we can feel that there is no hope. As we emerge from such times, it can be possible to develop a renewed understanding of what hope brings to our lives and world.

A common theme that emerges from responding to the questions posed in the activity below is the importance of family and friends in giving a person a sense of hope and belonging and informing a person's sense of identity and belonging – their sense of self. It is important to consider the profiles of the young people being worked with. For example, they may be 'looked after children' or asylum seekers and they may not have the same access to friends and family as other young

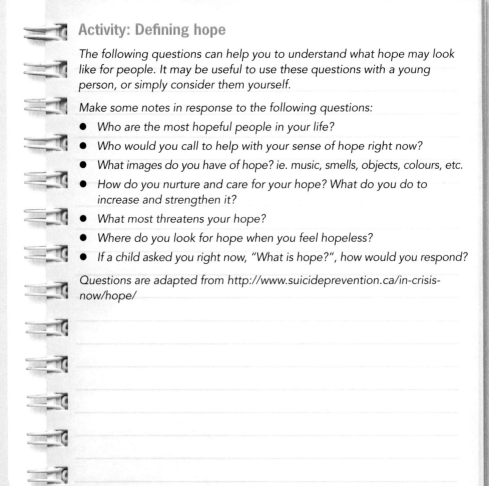

Activity: Defining hope

The following questions can help you to understand what hope may look like for people. It may be useful to use these questions with a young person, or simply consider them yourself.

Make some notes in response to the following questions:
- *Who are the most hopeful people in your life?*
- *Who would you call to help with your sense of hope right now?*
- *What images do you have of hope? ie. music, smells, objects, colours, etc.*
- *How do you nurture and care for your hope? What do you do to increase and strengthen it?*
- *What most threatens your hope?*
- *Where do you look for hope when you feel hopeless?*
- *If a child asked you right now, "What is hope?", how would you respond?*

Questions are adapted from http://www.suicideprevention.ca/in-crisis-now/hope/

people. Hope, how and where we learn to access it and importantly maintain it, is a critical part of how any child or adult's growing sense of self is shaped. Without it and/or the means to access it, despair and a sense of meaningless in the self can follow. This may mean that they are at an increased risk of considering suicide as a realistic choice.

Vaclav Havel was the Czech Republic's first president after the Velvet Revolution and he presided over the country's transition to democracy and a free market economy. Here is an extract from his obituary: 'A shot of [Vaclav] Havel with his back to the camera, walking toward the ocean – was turned into a poster and widely displayed around Prague, along with a quotation expressing one of Havel's most deeply held beliefs: "Hope is not the conviction that something will turn out well, but the certainty that something makes sense, regardless of how it turns out"' (Wilson, 2011).

The following poem muses on the importance of hope and how it can affect us:

'Hope; we ridicule those who have too much of it.

We hospitalize those who have too little.

It is dependent on so many things yet indisputably necessary to most.

Those who have it live longer.

Words cannot destroy it.

Science has overlooked it.

A day without it is dreadful.

A day with an abundance of it guarantees little.'

Reproduced with kind permission from Ronna Jevne (1991).

The language of suicide and its importance

As we know, stigma can have a negative impact on our sense of hope and so we need to consider how we can reduce the stigma while also increasing our understanding. Stigma can be perpetuated in communities. This is achieved not only through language but also through the various myths circulated within communities about why someone may come to die by suicide. Understanding these is an important first step in raising a local community's awareness and understanding about suicide. These steps need to be achieved to ensure they are incorporated into local suicide prevention strategies.

We have already touched on the language that has historically been used to describe suicide. P Bonny Ball argues that the term 'commit' suicide is not helpful or meaningful as it is outdated in its associations with criminality and it has its antecedents in the Middle Ages:

'"Committed suicide", "completed suicide" or "successful suicide" have historically been used to describe a death by suicide. The suicide prevention community is now realising that this language is **not accurate nor is it helpful.**

"Committed suicide", with its **implications of criminality, is a carry-over from the Middle Ages,** when civil authorities, finding the deceased beyond their reach, punished the survivors by confiscating their property. Those who died by suicide were forbidden traditional funerals and burials, and suicide was considered both illegal and sinful by the laws and religions of the time.

Today, the word "commit" presents a particular problem since it is also used for criminal offences such as homicide and assault.'
(Bonny Ball, 2011)

Reflection
- How do you feel about the person who dies by suicide?
- What do you think a person who dies by suicide is like?

Considering these questions will help you to challenge unhelpful myths about the act of suicide and those impacted by suicide.

Language can stigmatise particular groups. For example, people who are labelled as a 'refugee' may feel 'low', 'unrespected' and 'inferior' and be stigmatised or treated differently. In recent years, humanitarian and governmental agencies became aware that there was an increased number of suicides and attempted suicides among Bhutanese refugees in the camps in Nepal and among refugees resettled in the United States. The experience of being a refugee may cause a person to be displaced from their home and/ or family and friends, thus increasing the factors that may put them at risk of dying by suicide.

Figure 9 explores the link between suicide and stigma. Stigma arises from fear and ignorance about the act of suicide. This is very important as when a local area or school is developing youth suicide prevention guidelines, tackling stigma and considering the links shown on this diagram is vital.

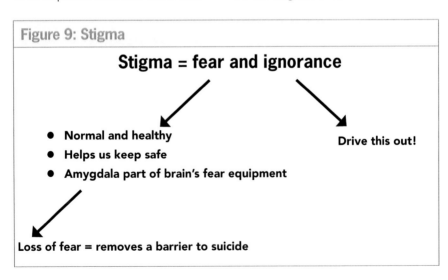

Figure 9: Stigma

Stigma = fear and ignorance

- **Normal and healthy**
- **Helps us keep safe**
- **Amygdala part of brain's fear equipment**

Drive this out!

Loss of fear = removes a barrier to suicide

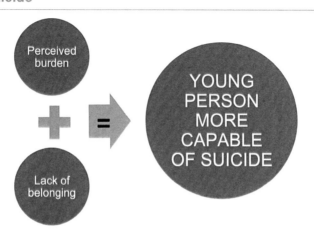

Figure 10: A model to understand thought processes and the act of suicide

Perceived burden

Lack of belonging

= YOUNG PERSON MORE CAPABLE OF SUICIDE

Myths about suicide

The next part of this section revisits myths about the 'suicidal mind' and the nature of suicide ie. what is the suicidal person thinking about?

Common myths about suicide include the following:

- **cowardice**
- weakness
- revenge
- **selfishness**
- self-centredness
- **impulsivity**.

Figure 10 offers a model to understand thought processes and the act of suicide. The two circles on the left represent the likely associated fears and situations of some people. It is the

Reflection

Consider the following features in relation to fear and the myth that suicide is about cowardice.

- People are fearful.
- Something that scares us is both fearful and daunting.
- We are wired to fear death.

Wouldn't it be difficult to be a coward and choose suicide?

combination of both these feelings that can lead to the circle on the right, which represents those who are capable of suicide becoming a reality.

Any local guidelines supporting prevention would need to consider how to reduce the presence of these factors in their organisational environments, as well as ensuring accessible resources and information is available to the young person who may be vulnerable. This is explored in more detail in the next section.

Fear and fearlessness

The amygdala is an almond-shaped mass of nuclei located deep within the temporal lobe of the brain. It is involved in the processing of emotions such as fear, anger and pleasure. The amygdala is also responsible for determining what memories are stored and where the memories are stored in the brain. It is thought that this determination is based on how big an emotional response an event invokes.

The amygdala is involved in several functions of the body including:

- arousal
- autonomic responses associated with fear
- emotional responses
- hormonal secretions
- memory.

What can professionals do to address a loss of physical fear?

Professionals need to create processes which encourage feelings of:

- connectedness
- purposefulness
- collectivity.

As a result of developments in neuroscience as evidenced in the ongoing work of Peter Levine (who developed the modality of treatment known as somatic experiencing as a way of working with children and adults who have experienced trauma/s recovery), we have been able to measure positive neurological changes and repair as a result of an increase in these three core areas.

Understanding and supporting the need for an inter-relationship between a person's mental and physiological development is critical, for example in the case of anorexia nervosa where early mortality is very high due to cardiac problems, conventional death and suicidal behaviour. The individual is physically fragile due to repeated starving. However, they will have trained themselves to be fearless of bodily matters and developed the power to control hunger. Box 6 summarises findings about mortality rates and anorexia nervosa.

> ### Box 6: Anorexia nervosa: mortality rates
>
> A meta-analysis of 36 studies into deaths from suicide in patients with anorexia nervosa and other eating disorders found that one in five individuals with anorexia nervosa had died by suicide. (Arcelus , 2011)
>
> A study by Holm-Denoma et al (2008) examined case reports of individuals with anorexia nervosa who had died by suicide. The study concluded that 'individuals with anorexia nervosa may habituate to the experience of pain during the course of their illness and accordingly die by suicide using methods that are highly lethal'.

Case study: Kurt Cobain

- Age 10–12: fear of needles, guns, the dark, spiders
- Witnessed increasing parental arguments – parents separated when he was about 9/10 years old
- Age 12–14: would not handle guns or go anywhere where they were present
- Age 16: got to like guns, went to shooting ranges, developed an active appetite for firearms
- Late teens/early 20s: became a frequent heroin user – lost earlier fear of needles

(Cross, 2001)

Kurt Cobain died aged 27 from self-inflicted gun shot.

Note the changes in Kurt Cobain's fears leading up to his suicide. The case study illustrates how Cobain was a fearful child who became less fearful (or overrode his fears) as he moved towards adulthood and his suicide.

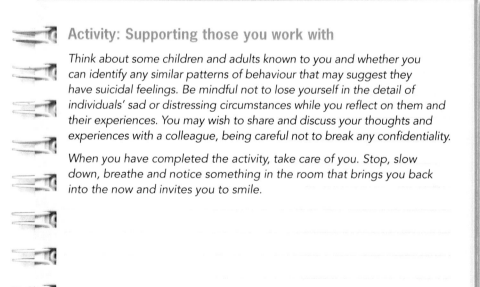

Activity: Supporting those you work with

Think about some children and adults known to you and whether you can identify any similar patterns of behaviour that may suggest they have suicidal feelings. Be mindful not to lose yourself in the detail of individuals' sad or distressing circumstances while you reflect on them and their experiences. You may wish to share and discuss your thoughts and experiences with a colleague, being careful not to break any confidentiality.

When you have completed the activity, take care of you. Stop, slow down, breathe and notice something in the room that brings you back into the now and invites you to smile.

Impulsivity

In considering the role of impulsivity in suicide, it is mistaken logic to assume impulsivity, since often the suicidal person is secretive in their premeditation. Humans are not wired to throw their lives away impulsively, although people get involved in impulsivity through higher risk activities eg. substance misuse.

Suicide is not impulsive; an individual will ruminate and prepare for suicide and then something will trigger the act. In suicide prevention there is a need to reduce the use of the word 'impulsivity' by replacing it with 'desire'. Certainly, some people have the 'desire' to die by suicide.

Selfishness

In 1905, the minister Samuel Miller said that suicide was an inherently selfish act: 'Suicide is generally

Reflection

Do you think taking your life by suicide is selfish? Myth or fact?

prompted by the most sordid and unworthy selfishness' (Kushner ,1989)

In December 2011, Jeremy Clarkson caused controversy by criticising people who kill themselves on train lines. He said that anyone who killed themselves in this way was 'very selfish' for traumatising train drivers and inconveniencing commuters (Daily Mail, 2011).

Interestingly, one definition of a psychopath is that they are inherently selfish yet few die by suicide.

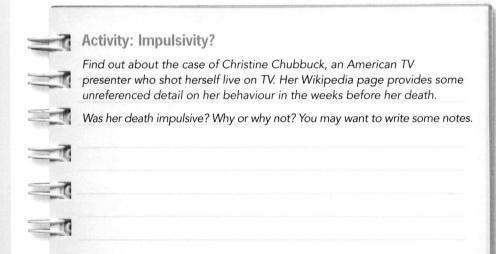

Activity: Impulsivity?

Find out about the case of Christine Chubbuck, an American TV presenter who shot herself live on TV. Her Wikipedia page provides some unreferenced detail on her behaviour in the weeks before her death.

Was her death impulsive? Why or why not? You may want to write some notes.

What to listen for?

The combination of the two perceptions the child below expresses increases their risk of dying by suicide.

The case study above goes back to the idea introduced in Figure 10 on page 77 when a young person has a belief that they are a burden to others and/or has a sense of not belonging. The presence of both is when the young person may be at greater risk of suicide.

Note the move from the negative observations of self to believing that their existence is also negative for others ie. they are a burden.

How can a worker identify the presence of these feelings in a young person? The case study above gives examples of the way the teenage boy talks about his feelings of self eg. 'I hate myself' and 'I am terrible'. He then goes onto say: 'There's no point me hanging around here ruining people's lives'. This illustrates how the boy's dislike of self is in his mind being projected back at him by his perception of others' actions and behaviours – however real or not the behaviours of others may or may not be

to the child, they are feeling not needed or wanted. The combination of both perceptions by the child increases his risk of dying by suicide.

Transactional Analysis and understanding how people function

Transactional Analysis can help us to understand how people function and how they express their personality in terms of behaviour.

During a pilot session on this topic by the author, a worker asked about a child they had been working with for some time. The child self-harmed, had suicidal ideation and was convinced that they were 'useless' and there was no point in anything. The worker asked how someone could come to hold such a negative view of themself, and how was it that they were struggling to shift the young person's view of self. The Parent-Adult-Child model from Transactional Analysis offers a useful model to start to consider a professional's understanding of what might be contributing to a child feeling suicidal.

Figure 11: Introducing the Parent-Adult-Child model

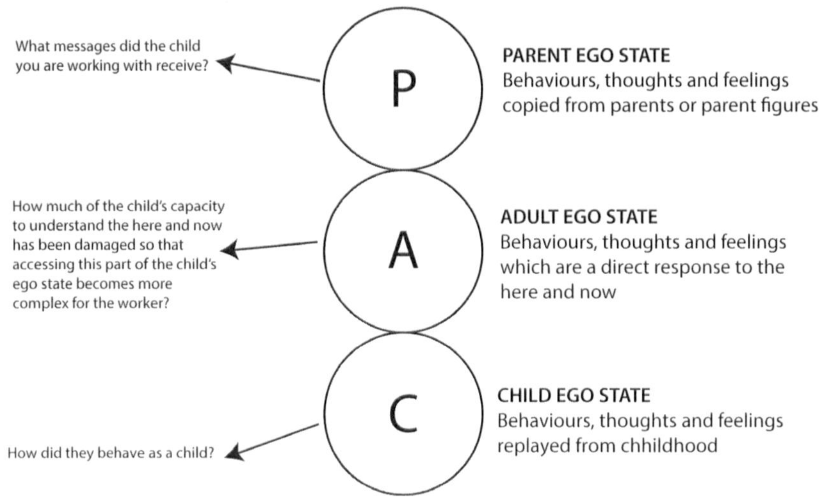

What messages did the child you are working with receive?

P

PARENT EGO STATE
Behaviours, thoughts and feelings copied from parents or parent figures

How much of the child's capacity to understand the here and now has been damaged so that accessing this part of the child's ego state becomes more complex for the worker?

A

ADULT EGO STATE
Behaviours, thoughts and feelings which are a direct response to the here and now

C

CHILD EGO STATE
Behaviours, thoughts and feelings replayed from chhildhood

How did they behave as a child?

Transactional Analysis can help us to understand how people function and how they express their personality in terms of behaviour. The following offers a simplified, but useful summary which in itself can offer a basic framework to support this work.

In order to use a Transactional Analysis framework you need to have a basic understanding of the ego. In Transactional Analysis an ego state is a set of related behaviours informed by three parts, usually illustrated as three separate circles placed one on top of another. Each circle has one of the following capital letters, PAC, placed inside it, and this led to it being referenced as the PAC Model.

To expand, if a person is behaving, thinking and feeling in response to what is happening now, they are said to be in their Adult ego state. This is depicted as an A in the middle circle.

The other two ego states are known as Parent and Child. The former results in behaviours induced by certain stimuli, resulting in us copying the behaviours of our childhood carers (be these negative or positive); the latter is when we return to the behaviours we adopted as children, again, usually provoked by certain stimuli, be it another's behaviour towards us or an environmental factor.

Behaviours learnt and held within the Parent and Child ego states of a young person who is suicidal can cause the Adult ego state to be difficult for the young person to access. For example, the Parent ego and the Child ego may be more developed than the Adult ego, as shown in the Child model in Figure

Figure 12: The child in relation to the worker

The Child

The child has difficulty accessing their adult ego state.

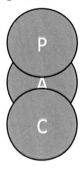

The Worker

The worker has difficulty accessing the child's adult ego state.

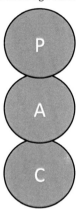

12. This may cause the young person to replay negative messages they received from their parents or carers and behave as they did as a young child in response to them. It may cause a child to replay messages that they are worthless or feel hopeless. As a result, a professional may find it difficult to access the young person's Adult ego state to support them when they feel suicidal.

Stigma and myths

Some communities – schools, prisons and residential settings – are often environments in which bullying and fearlessness can be perpetuated through peer pressure and culture. Therefore, it is important to consider the potential impact if these environments do not address this within youth suicide prevention programmes. Suicide prevention programmes need to focus on dispelling myths, like the following:

Myth: Confronting a person about suicide will only make them angry and increase the risk of suicide.

Fact: Asking someone directly about suicidal intent lowers anxiety, opens up communication, and lowers the risk of an impulsive act.

Myth: Only experts can prevent suicide.

Fact: Suicide prevention is everybody's business, and anyone can help prevent the tragedy of suicide.

Suicide prevention programmes should focus on the following warning signs.

Children and young people feeling:

- alienated
- lonely
- lacking in hope
- fearless
- they are lacking in a sense of belonging
- they are a burden.

The aim should be to create organisational systems to reduce and address such feelings leading to a healthy community and peer cultures.

Reflective practice questions

Reflect on the content of Section 5 and the issues it has raised for you on both personal and professional levels.
- What are the key learning points for you?
- What aspects of your learning will you take into your practice?
- What needs for continuing professional development have you identified, if any?

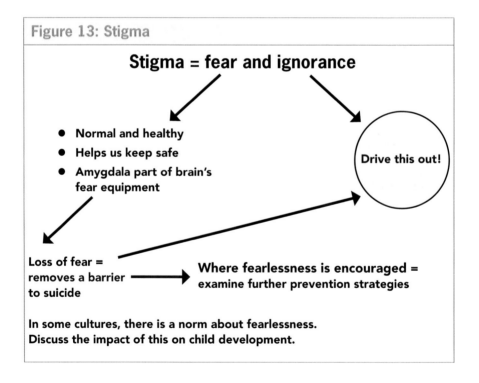

Figure 13: Stigma

Stigma = fear and ignorance

- **Normal and healthy**
- **Helps us keep safe**
- **Amygdala part of brain's fear equipment**

Drive this out!

Loss of fear = removes a barrier to suicide

Where fearlessness is encouraged = examine further prevention strategies

In some cultures, there is a norm about fearlessness. Discuss the impact of this on child development.

References

Arcelus J, Mitchell A, Wales J & Nielsen S (2011) Mortality rates in patients with anorexia nervosa and other eating disorders: a meta-analysis of 36 studies. *Archives of General Psychiatry* **68** (7) 724–731.

Bonny Ball P (2011) *The Power of Words – the language of suicide* [online]. Available at: http://www.yourlifecounts.org/blog/article-bonny-ball-power-words (accessed January 2015).

Cross C (2001) *Heavier Than Heaven: A biography of Kurt Cobain*. New York: Hyperion.

Daily Mail (2011) *Clarkson strikes again: Now TV presenter brands suicide victims 'very selfish'* [online]. Available at: http://www.dailymail.co.uk/news/article-2069493/Jeremy-Clarkson-brands-suicide-victims-selfish.html# ixzz2F2f0fGdw.

Holm-Denoma JM, Witte JK, Gordon KH, Herzog DB, Franko DL, Fitchter M, Quadflieg N & Joiner TE (2008) Deaths by suicide among individuals with anorexia as arbiters between competing explanations of the anorexia-suicide link. *Journal of Affective Disorders* **107** (1–3) 231–236.

Jevne R (1991) *It All Begins With Hope: Patients, caregivers and the bereaved speak out*. San Diego: Lura Media.

Kushner H (1989) *American Suicide: A psychocultural exploration*. New Brunswick: Rutgers University Press.

Wilson P (2011) Vaclav Havel's obituary. Available via subscription at: http://www.nybooks.com/articles/archives/2012/feb/09/vaclav-havel-1936-2011/?page=2 (accessed January 2015).

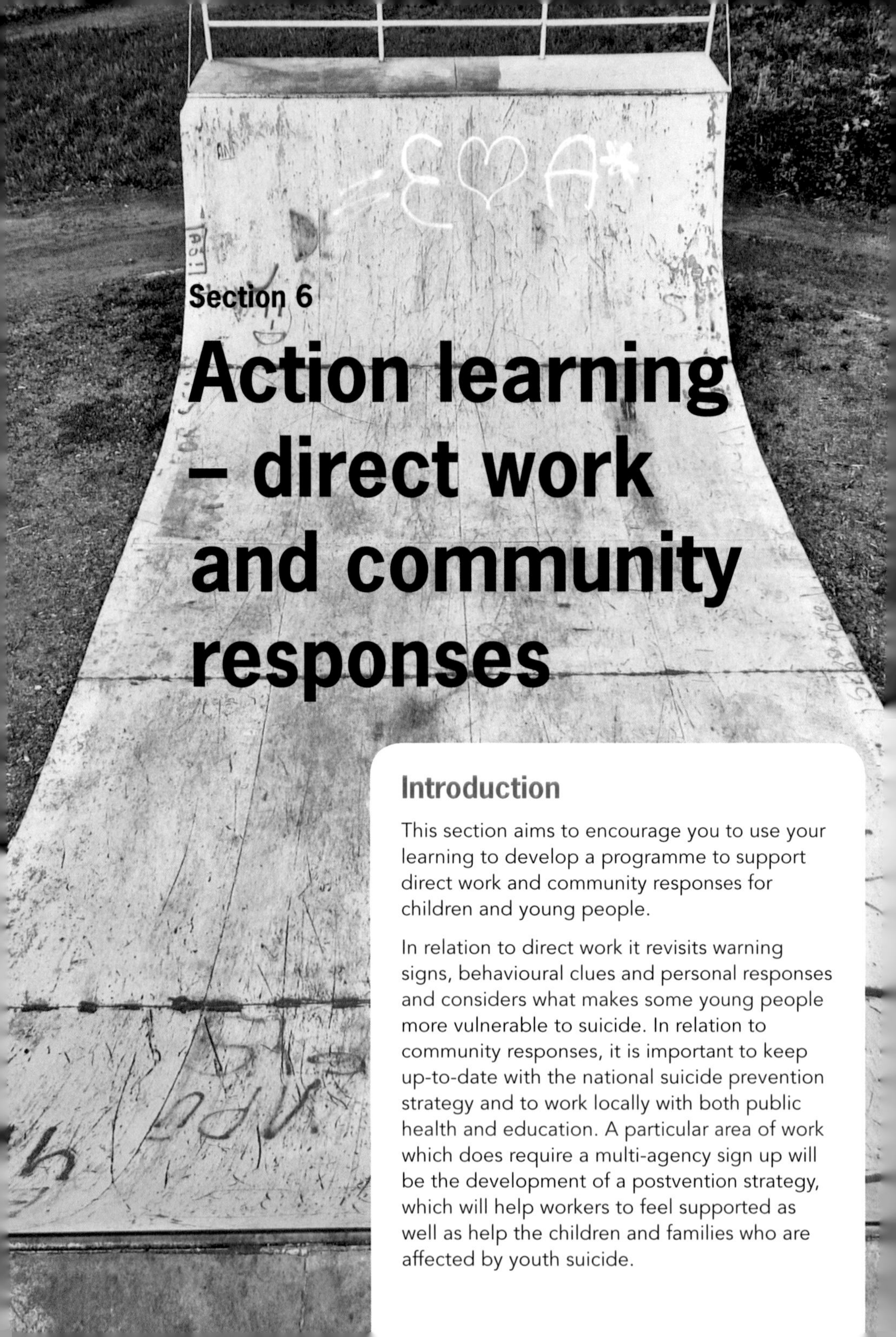

Action learning – direct work and community responses

Introduction

This section aims to encourage you to use your learning to develop a programme to support direct work and community responses for children and young people.

In relation to direct work it revisits warning signs, behavioural clues and personal responses and considers what makes some young people more vulnerable to suicide. In relation to community responses, it is important to keep up-to-date with the national suicide prevention strategy and to work locally with both public health and education. A particular area of work which does require a multi-agency sign up will be the development of a postvention strategy, which will help workers to feel supported as well as help the children and families who are affected by youth suicide.

Supporting direct work

A person's thought cycle can make them more vulnerable to suicide and they may display warning signs, which need to be addressed if they are contemplating suicide.

You will need to consider:

- what is the vulnerable person's thought process?
- are there any warning signs?
- how to address the warning signs.

Reflection

What can you remember about the Parent-Adult-Child ego model that was covered in Section 5? How does it help to address the points below?

Transactional Analysis and the vulnerable young person

This sub-section explores the use of Transactional Analysis in more detail to support work in developing a potential model of the vulnerable person's thought cycle.

The model is introduced here to help understand how a young person's developing ego states are impacted by early childhood messages from their carers, and how these in turn can be perpetuated by the child's interactions with others. In Section 5, the Parent-Adult-Child model was introduced to encourage you to think about how a child who feels they do not belong and are a burden to others might come to develop a view of themselves as being 'I'm not OK'.

The Parent-Adult-Child model asserts that we each internalise models of parents, children and adults, and that we play these roles out within our own developing selves and with one another in our relationships. The model poses two forms of Parent; the Controlling Parent and the Nurturing Parent. It is important to see these two forms as appearing at either end of a spectrum. Many people will have experiences of less extreme versions, but some can have experiences of the extremes, and it is the experience of the former which can have unhelpful implications for the child's developing ego states.

The Nurturing Parent is caring and concerned, and often may appear as a mother figure, though men can play it too. They seek to keep the Child contented, offering a safe haven and unconditional love to calm the Child's troubles. This can be positive and negative as it can lead to a completely hands off parenting style.

The Controlling (or Critical) Parent tries to make the Child do as the parent wants them to do, perhaps transferring values or beliefs, or helping the Child to understand and live in society. They may also have a more negative intent.

The messages informing the Adult ego are behaviours, thoughts and feelings which are direct responses to the here and now. The Adult in us is the 'grown up' rational person who talks reasonably and assertively, neither trying to control nor reacting aggressively towards others. The Adult is comfortable with themself and is where we need to be when transacting with another in a healthy, positive way. Transactional Analysis proposes three types of Child.

The Child ego state is the part of our personality that holds the emotions, thoughts, and feelings experienced by ourselves from childhood. We carry around in our Child ego state all the experiences we have had, and sometimes these childlike ways of being are repeated in our adult relationships. This can be fun when we are in a situation in which it is safe and right to play and enjoy ourselves. It can be a problem when our Child view of the world causes us to distort the facts in a current situation and prevents our Adult ego state from seeing things accurately. This is very important to understand when working with a young person who may have some distorted thoughts about themselves as a result of these childhood experiences and memories.

Understanding which of the three types of Child ego state is dominant in the young person is very important.

Transactional Analysis refers to the three ego states as the Free Child (natural ego state), the Adaptive Child and the Little Professor.

When two people communicate, each exchange is a transaction. Many of our problems come from transactions which are unsuccessful. People can unwittingly 'play games' as a result of their transactions, both within their own understanding of the people and situations, as well as with one another. Many games between these positions begin to reinforce how people make sense of the world.

The transactions between a young person and their carers can give us a great deal of insight into how the young person makes sense of their world and has grown to perceive their own sense of self either positively or negatively. These transactions become 'wired' within the child's developing sense of self and are called scripts. Scripts can be positive and give us a sense of control and identity and reassure us that all is still well in the world. Where this is not the case, the young person can seek out games which are negative and destructive and play them more out of sense of habit and addiction than constructive pleasure. Scripts may be responsible for a child's lack of belonging or sense of being a burden.

Complementary transactions occur when both people are at the same level ie. Parent talking to Parent etc. Here, both are often thinking in the same way and communication is easier. Problems usually occur in crossed transactions, where each person is talking to a different ego level. The parent is either nurturing or controlling, and often speaks to the child, who is either adaptive or 'natural' in their response. When both people talk as a Parent to the other's Child, their wires get crossed and conflict results. The ideal line of communication is the mature and rational Adult-Adult relationship and this is what workers should strive to achieve when supporting a young person.

Box 7 looks at the injunctions and drivers in a person's thought cycle. The definitions of these are in Box 8.

The vulnerable young person will have some of these views about themselves. In Transactional Analysis these views are separated out and referred to as injunctions and drivers. Having an understanding of these can help both the professional and young person understand the negative patterns which can keep the young person in an unhappy and distressed state.

Figure 14 illustrates the thought process a young person may have and where it can lead.

It is the role of schools and environments in which children are present to intervene to challenge a faulty belief system.

Box 7: Understanding the vulnerable person's thought cycle

Injunctions	Drivers
• Negative, restrictive script • Messages issued from the Child ego by the Parent ego and housed in Child ego (messages that imbed into a child's beliefs and life script)	One of five distinctive behavioural sequences (be perfect, please others, try hard, be strong and hurry up) we can play out and are functional manifestations of negative counterscripts

(Stewart & Jones, 2007)

Box 8: A vulnerable person may struggle with injunctions and drivers

Injunctions	Drivers
• Don't feel – anger/sexual • Don't exist • Don't be you • Don't grow up • Don't be important	• Be perfect • Please others • Be strong • Try hard • Hurry up

How do some children or young people end up feeling 'I'm not OK'?

Children and young people start out in life as being 'I'm OK – You're OK'. They then learn patterns of behaving as a 'script' via the positive and negative messages they receive from others. They then continue to seek out those repeated messages.

Reflection

What do you think the warning signs that a person is thinking about dying by suicide might be?

Figure 14: A vulnerable person's cycle – working with a belief cycle

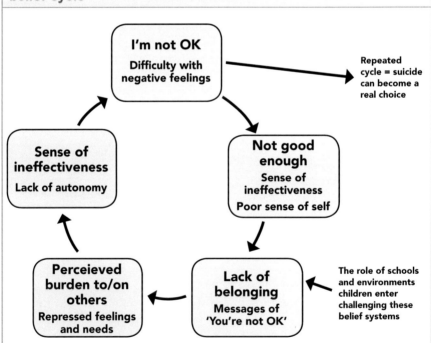

I'm not OK
Difficulty with negative feelings

Repeated cycle = suicide can become a real choice

Not good enough
Sense of ineffectiveness
Poor sense of self

Sense of ineffectiveness
Lack of autonomy

Perceieved burden to/on others
Repressed feelings and needs

Lack of belonging
Messages of 'You're not OK'

The role of schools and environments children enter challenging these belief systems

It is important to take the warning signs of youth suicide seriously and to seek help if you think you know a teenager who might be suicidal.

Box 9 lists general warning signs. More specific warning signs are listed in Box 10.

Here are some general tips on approaching a young person if they are considering suicide:

- If in doubt, don't wait, ask the question.
- If the young person doesn't want to talk, be persistent.
- Talk to the young person alone in a private setting or ask if the young person wants to have the conversation with a family member or friend present.
- Ask the young person if they want an interpreter to be present.
- Allow the young person to talk freely.
- Give yourself plenty of time.

Box 9: General warning signs

- Talking about wanting to die or killing oneself
- Looking for a way to kill oneself, such as doing research online
- Talking about feeling hopeless or having no reason to live
- Talking about feeling trapped or in unbearable pain
- Talking about being a burden to others

- Increasing the use of alcohol or drugs
- Acting anxious or agitated; behaving recklessly
- Sleeping too little or too much
- Withdrawing or feeling isolated
- Showing rage or talking about seeking revenge
- Displaying extreme mood swings

Adapted from NIMH (2014)

Box 10: More specific warning signs

- Disinterest in hobbies
- Problems at work and losing interest in a task
- Substance abuse including alcohol and drug use
- Behavioural problems
- Withdrawing from family and friends
- Changes in sleeping patterns
- Changes in eating habits
- Neglecting hygiene and personal appearance

- Physical complaints eg. aches, fatigue, migraines
- Difficulty concentrating
- Decline in the standard of school work
- Loss of interest in school
- Risk taking behaviours
- Complaining more frequently of boredom
- Not responding to praise

Adapted from Teen Suicide (2005)

Remember: how you ask the question is less important than the fact that you ask it.

Some direct verbal clues that a person is considering suicide offer a direct approach to asking the question:

- 'I've decided to kill myself.'
- 'I wish I were dead.'
- 'I'm going to commit suicide.'
- 'I'm going to end it all.'
- 'If (such and such) doesn't happen, I'll kill myself.'

Examples of direct responses to a young person's indication that they may be considering suicide could include:

- 'You know, when people are as upset as you seem to be they sometimes wish they were dead. I'm wondering if you're feeling that way, too?'
- 'You seem pretty miserable, I wonder if you're thinking about suicide?'
- 'Are you thinking about killing yourself?'

Important: If you cannot ask the question, find someone who can.

Indirect clues that a person is considering suicide could include:

- 'I'm tired of life, I just can't go on'
- 'My family would be better off without me'
- 'Who cares if I'm dead anyway'
- 'I just want out'
- 'I won't be around much longer'
- 'Pretty soon, you won't have to worry about me'

Examples of a less direct approach to asking about suicide could be:

- 'Have you been unhappy lately?'
- 'Have you been very unhappy lately?'
- 'Have you been so unhappy lately that you've been thinking about ending your life?'
- 'Do you ever wish you could go to sleep and never wake up?'

In supporting a child who is contemplating suicide:

- listen to their problems and give them your full attention
- remember, suicide is not the problem, only the solution to a problem that a person thinks cannot be solved
- do not rush to judge or find a solution
- offer hope in any form.

Box 11 details some suggested responses to common warning signs.

Box 11: How to respond warning signs

- Develop a suicide prevention community response
- Give peers more information as the majority of young people turn to their friends first for advice
- Increase educational programmes for young people
- Increase student knowledge of warning signs
- Have a well advertised hotline number readily available
- Provide children with meaningful roles within youth organisations
- Ask children direct questions
- Talking about suicide in the classroom gives an avenue to talk about feelings
- Acknowledge and openly discuss the subject
- A lot of a child's feelings are connected to their school

The acronym IS PATH WARM?, created by the American Association of Suicidology, can be used as a mnemonic to remember the warning signs of suicide:

Ideation: Threatened or communicated

Substance abuse: Excessive or increased

Purposeless: No reasons for living

Anxiety: Agitation/insomnia

Trapped: Feeling there is no way out

Hopelessness

Withdrawing: From friends, family, society

Anger (uncontrolled): Rage, seeking revenge

Recklessness: Risky acts, unthinking

Mood changes (dramatic)

Reflection

How will you take your learning forward into your work and your community?

- experience an impact on their sense of belonging in the community
  - be more vulnerable to PTSD (due to complex grief process)
- experience a heightened sensitivity to fearful vs. fearlessness.

Community responses

Postvention

A postvention describes a process to support schools and/or other children's services when responding to a completed, attempted or suspected suicide within a pupil community or an organisation. Postvention aims to support communities:

- in grief
- responding to the risk of suicide contagion
- responding to and working with the media.

In achieving these aims, it is important that there is sensitive sharing of information across and between schools, between children's services, CAMHS and families. Postvention guidelines need to form part of local safeguarding policies and protocols.

The impact of suicide on family and friends can be far-reaching. Survivors can:

- feel dishonourable
- stigmatise their grief

Examples of community action taken forward in the UK and other countries includes the following:

- closer collaboration with the media ie. guidelines for responsible reporting
- the Netherlands and Austria encourage responsible dissemination of information on suicide
- preventing suicide at hotspots, promoting research on suicide prevention (in England)
- Canada has developed the 'Pillars for Building a Suicide Safe Community' involving six elements to support community action including leadership, an action plan, training, mental health promotion, bereavement, postvention network
- Ireland, Scotland, Wales and Austria have a strong focus on stigma reduction
- Scotland and Wales focus on attitudes towards suicide.

References

NIMH (2014) Some common questions and answers about suicide [online]. Available at: http://www.nimh.nih.gov/health/publications/suicide-a-major-preventable-mental-health-problem-fact-sheet/suicide-a-major-preventable-mental-health-problem.shtml (accessed January 2015).

Stewart and Jones (2007) *TA Today: A new introduction to transactional analysis* (3rd edition). Nottingham: Chapel Hill.

Teen Suicide (2005) Teen suicide warning signs [online]. Available at: http://www.teensuicide.us/articles2.html (accessed January 2015).

Reflective practice questions

Reflect on the content of Section 6 and the issues it has raised for you on both personal and professional levels.
- What are the key learning learning points for you?
- What aspects of your learning will you take into your practice?
- What needs for continuing professional development have you identified, if any?

Further resources

Sellen J (2013) *Encouraging Reflective Practice: Action Learning Pack.* Impact Wellbeing.

A concluding note from the author

Since the early 1980s, I have worked alongside people who self-harm and/or with those who have been affected by those who self-harm or consider suicide, or who have ended their relationship with themselves by suicide. Over the past few years statistics have shown a drop in actual numbers and then increases followed by drops. There have also been epidemiological changes. However, people are still choosing to take their lives, and this is hard for many to make sense of, comprehend and recover from.

Many more children are scratching and making both small and large incisions into parts of their bodies, and we keep asking them and ourselves the same questions. My invitation to us all is to ask new questions and recognise that the role and function of both self-harm and suicide for some has changed, and those of us working in the field need to change with it.

In this guide I have invited you to rethink the old mantra that self-harm is a 'coping strategy' and replace it with the idea that self-harm supports 'mood alteration'. Why? Because in my experience many young people and children do not know why they self-harm; their understanding is increasingly constructed not within their relationship with carers, or indeed friends, but with the internet. Google or other internet search engines are constructed and informed by the attitudes of those who create them.

Yes, coping is a quality, but it also carries a lot of connotations frequently associated with the profile of a victim. Reducing either yourself or being viewed as a victim is arguably unhealthy and dangerous.

Some children and young people who self-harm may well have been victims of abuse, crime, domestic violence, bullying and so forth, but they are not victims per se. Most came into the world as passionate, strong, warm, thoughtful, insightful children whose capacity to access these qualities has for a range of reasons diminished and for some become barely visible. The concept of mood alteration invites us and those we work with to revisit and see the ways in which self-harming behaviours are a choice to alter mood.

Most of you reading this are in the business of mood alteration and you work with children and young people to support them manage their feelings in healthy, social and personally positive ways. Recognising a child as self-harming to alter their mood invites both us and them to view them as someone who is making a choice – they are an actor rather than a puppet in their world. Circumstances may well have contributed to many feeling out of control and being reactive rather than proactive.

The role and function of self-harm in my view has arguably changed, while for some these will be the same, for many of our children in schools and communities across Britain we need to take heed from the increasing body of knowledge in neuroscience. Advancements in technology, the pace of change, the increase in stimuli and expectations of use placed upon a child's developing brain cannot in my view be ignored in making sense of why children self-harm, contemplate suicide and actually may die by suicide.

Put simply, the overuse of the neo-cortex part of the brain, in contrast with the lack of support to the limbic parts of the brain and the potential for the reptilian part of the brain to be over alert, leads to many children feeling like someone is pulling one end of a piece of elastic while another is pulling the other end. The result is heightened anxiety, increased inability to cope with change, increased need for order and/or outbursts of anger or withdrawal. Using the external parts of the body to communicate these confounding and frustrating contradictions is arguably, for many children, just that, a form of communication. The question is do we understand what they are telling us?

Jude

Useful contacts

42nd Street

42nd Street works with young people 13–25 living in Manchester, Salford and Trafford and provides a range of services including counselling, individual support, group work and volunteering opportunities.

Web: http://42ndstreet.org.uk/

Helpline: 0161 2281888

Fax: 0161 2280528

Email: theteam@42ndstreet.org.uk

Address: 42nd Street, the SPACE, 87–91 Great Ancoats Street, Manchester M4 5AG

Aware Defeat Depression

'We do more for the one in four with depression in Northern Ireland.'

Web: www.aware-ni.org

Phone: 08451 202961

Email: help@aware-ni.org

Bristol Crisis Service for Women

Bristol Crisis Service for Women was set up in 1986 to respond to the needs of women in emotional distress. It has a focus on self-injury and has carried out extensive research. It provides a range of information and publications on self-injury and training for professionals. It has specific information for young women, women from black and minority ethnic groups (information published in Bengali, Chinese, English, Punjabi and Urdu) and women in prison.

Website: www.selfinjurysupport.org.uk

Text: 07800 472 908 (text service for girls and young women (11-25). Monday to Friday, 7–9pm.

Address: Bristol Crisis Service for Women, PO Box 654, Bristol BS99 1XH

British Association for Counselling and Psychotherapy

BACP is a professional body representing counselling and psychotherapy, and works towards a better standard of therapeutic practice.

Website: www.bacp.co.uk

Phone: 0870 443 5252

Centre for Suicide Research

The Centre focuses on the investigation of the causes, treatment and prevention of suicidal behaviour.

Website: http://cebmh.warne.ox.ac.uk/csr/

ChildLine

Website: www.childline.org

Phone: 0800 1111

Get Connected – website for young people

Web: www.getconnected.org.uk/

Phone: 0808 808 4994

Impact Wellbeing

Impact Wellbeing is a non-profit social enterprise committed to tackling the impact of trauma on children and young people to reduce self-harm and suicide as a choice. Workshops, reflective practice, film making, supervision and bespoke programmes are available for individuals, groups, schools and services in communities UK-wide. All available to young people, families and professionals.

Web: www.impactwellbeing.org.uk

Facebook: www.facebook.com/impactwellbeing

Phone: 01273 844194

Email: jude@wellbeingprojects.co.uk (founder) or edwina@wellbeingprojects.co.uk (programme director)

Mind

Mind offers advice and support to anyone affected by a mental health problem.

Web: www.mind.org.uk/help/advice_lines

Phone: 020 8519 2122

Email: contact@mind.org.uk

Address: 15–19 Broadway, Stratford, London E15 4BQ

National Self Harm Network

A UK charity offering support, advice and advocacy services to people affected by self-harm directly or in a care role.

Web: www.nshn.co.uk

NHS 111

NHS 111 is for when you need medical help fast but it's not a 999 emergency. The service is available 24 hours a day, 365 days a year. Calls are free from landlines and mobile phones.

Website: http://www.nhs.uk/NHSEngland/AboutNHSservices/Emergencyandurgentcareservices/Pages/NHS-111.aspx

Phone: 111

PAPYRUS Prevention of Young Suicide

PAPYRUS was founded in 1997 by Jean Kerr, a mother from Lancashire. She and a small group of parents who had each lost a child to suicide were convinced that many young suicides are preventable.

Address: 67 Bewsey Street, Warrington, Cheshire, WA2 7JQ

Website: papyrus-uk.org

Phone: 01925 572 444 (Monday to Friday 9am to 5pm)

Confidential help and support line: 0800 0684141

Fax: 01925 240 502

Samaritans

Available 24 hours a day providing confidential emotional support for people experiencing feelings of distress, despair or suicidal thoughts.

Web: www.samaritans.org

Phone: 08457 909090 (UK) 1850 60 90 90* (ROI)

Email: jo@samaritans.org

Write: Freepost RSRB-KKBY-CYJK, Chris, PO Box 90 90, Stirling, FK8 2SA

Saneline

Saneline is a national helpline providing information and support for people with mental health problems and those who support them.

Website: www.sane.org.uk

Phone: 0845 767 8000

Self-harm in primary schools: what you can do

Website: http://www.optimus-education.com/tackling-self-harm-primary-schools (subscription needed)

The Site

Advice for young people on self-harm and recovery

Website: www.thesite.org/healthandwellbeing/mentalhealth/selfharm

Survivors of Bereavement by Suicide (SOBS)

SOBS aims to provide a safe, confidential environment in which bereaved people can share their experiences and feelings.

Website: www.uk-sobs.org.uk

Phone: 0844 561 6855

YoungMinds

YoungMinds is the UK's leading charity committed to improving the emotional well-being and mental health of children and young people. Driven by their experiences, it campaigns, researches and influences policy and practice.

Web: www.youngminds.org.uk

Phone: 020 7089 5050

Email for parents with concerns about a child: parents@youngminds.org.uk

Email for general enquiries: ymenquiries@youngminds.org.uk

Address: Suite 11, Baden Place, Crosby Row, London, SE1 1YW

Notes

Notes